To Michael
best wishes
Ian Delmoré
July 2009.

Coconuts Kill More People Than Sharks

DAVID DEL MONTÉ

AuthorHouse™ UK Ltd.
500 Avebury Boulevard
Central Milton Keynes, MK9 2BE
www.authorhouse.co.uk
Phone: 08001974150

© 2009 DAVID DEL MONTÉ. All rights reserved.

No part of this book may be reproduced, stored in a retrieval system, or transmitted by any means without the written permission of the author.

First published by AuthorHouse 5/14/2009

ISBN: 978-1-4389-5128-7 (sc)
ISBN: 978-1-4389-5504-9 (hc)

Printed in the United States of America
Bloomington, Indiana

This book is printed on acid-free paper.

To M.D, G.D., H.D., T.D., and M.L. (begetter of my joys)

Preface

Some of these tales were written to entertain myself, at home, or whilst travelling. But most of them were written because they had to be. I have enjoyed writing stories from an early age. But I come from an Anglo-Jewish family for whom success in business is more of a requisite than literary skill. So, until now, I have been a reclusive writer, which stems from my inhibition in inhabiting that coveted role. I preferred to march out into the world to make my way, to 'present' the shining face of a successful man. To satisfy what was expected of me, and of course, what I expected of myself.

Although at 'A' level I enjoyed the decoding of *Dubliners*, an astonishingly mature work by the young Joyce, I did not enjoy the forensic literary criticism at university with its incessant cliquiness and feuds. I turned to theatre instead. But I always wrote prose, much of it, mercifully, that was not good enough to 'walk', or work.

Because writing is a muscle; the more you do it, the better it gets. Many of these stories were set down early in the morning, shortly after waking. Often the germ of the idea was a dream, or a thought.

Some went through many drafts of re-writing, others hardly at all. Technically I improved the more I wrote, but this does not mean I was always possessed of an superhuman energy that would lead me through from the beginning of the story to the end, with the characters driving it on. Stories such as 'Life-Swap' began as an idea many years ago, but only came through as a finished product much later. All this goes to show, I think, is that the writing process is a mystery, which has yet to be fully divined.

I am not an atheist in the sense that I know that the universe does not obey random laws. Life is too extraordinary for it to have come about by accident. There is a pattern, but to date, the complexity defeats us. When the witting is going well it almost seems that there is an other than human source for inspiration. But the explanation of all these things is still out of our reach, and it is precisely the kind of exploration that we do when we read that makes our voyage, if the writing is good, so wonderful.

On this portentous note it is time for you to turn the page, and begin your journey.

David Del Monté, Almaty, April 2009
eburyee@aol.com

Contents

Preface	vii
LIFE SWAP	1
THE TREATMENT	20
COCONUTS KILL MORE PEOPLE THAN SHARKS	38
QUANTUCK LUBECK'S INHERITANCE	48
A DREAM OF WILSON PICKETT'S	54
THE MAN WHO KEPT PANTHERS	68
ANIMAL RIGHTS	74
THE ANCHORITE OF GLASSFIBREVILLE	80
HONORARY CONSUL	84
HOUSE	93
MRS PHARAOH	101
BOATMAN	121
ONE FOR THE ROAD	132
THE SWITCH	146
SELLING UP	156
GYM MASTERS	164
THE DEATH OF MR KAY	179
GHOST STORY	195
VALENTINE	207
JUDE – JEW	229
ADRIAN	237
WASTE NOT WANT NOT	243
DR PLOV	253

LIFE SWAP

When my friend Jasper, the art student, told me that he wanted to do a life swap with someone for one month to mark his crowning achievement as an artist, I was not surprised. The previous year he had been a Golden Labrador for one day, dressed up in a furry canine suit. He ate tinned Miller's Beef chunks with raw marrowbone from a dog bowl on the floor. Remaining for the entire twenty-four hours on all fours and attached to a lead, he had been taken to chase after pigeons in Trafalgar Square. Hoisting up one hind leg, he had peed on parked cars, pillar boxes, and the highly polished boot of a sentry standing to attention in Horse Guards Parade. His poo had been 'scooped' by his handler and deposited in the dog-litter bins in Princes Park, and the police had been called to deal with two old ladies who had fainted at the sight. The constables were not amused by the man in the dog suit with the lolling tongue and wagging tail, and it needed the personal intervention of Jasper's tutor, who arrived in a battered yellow Datsun fresh from his early morning workout at the Virgin Health club, to ensure that Jasper was not carted away and charged with indecency in a public place. Yes, Jasper certainly pushed the boundaries of art.

His latest idea was going to count towards his final degree as an artist.

As you can see, Jasper was not an artist in the traditional sense, but he had plenty of concepts, which is what passes for art these days.

The life swap concept quickly gained the acceptance of his tutors. In fact, he was earmarked for a First, everyone said. He also set up a replica of his bedsit, which he built in the lobby of the art school here in Dipcaster (pronounced Dip'ster), replete with three live mice running under the floorboards. Two of the mice were inadvertently poisoned by the janitor, who did not realise they were art, and the other was killed by the college cat. Jasper videoed the mouse being tossed about inside the cat's jaws. It was a bit sickening, if you ask me. He also photographed the janitor, whose bristly face resembled the ravaged look of an Okie from the Great Depression of the 1930s. The act of setting it all up owed more to the skills of a man with a jigsaw and a piece of MDF plywood than it did to adroitness with a brush or palette.

So when I went into my depression it was Jasper to whom I turned rather than my girlfriend, Sue, who was heavily into counselling herself and unable to listen to anybody, despite the fact that she liked to talk about her past and her issues with me well into the early hours of the morning. She lost track of time, she said.

We did not live together as her place was far away, but sometimes our late-night conversations drifted towards sex. 'I'm naked,' she would say, 'in bed, and I look great. How about you?'

'Yes, I am naked too,' I would say.

There would then come a pause, and then she'd say 'Tell me a secret.'

If I replied honestly, it would be to say 'I have a hard-on,' but if I told her this, she'd slam down the phone and call Marcia, who would castigate me as phallicentric and advise Sue to break off all relations with me. Marcia has a PhD in psychology. She is black, wears dreadlocks, and Sue always listens to her. Marcia has already 'red-flagged' me to Sue as a pervert. I wanted to tell Sue that this was because Marcia was a man-hating flathead who was Sue's worst nightmare, but Marcia was Sue's best friend.

'A secret?' I would say, 'Hmm, I can't think of any.' I wish she had said, 'Lie on top of me and imagine you are having sex with me', and we could both get off at the same time, but no. She would just chunder on about how much she weighed and what her breasts looked like. And then she'd say 'Love to meet you', but she never did. She has always been a virtual girlfriend.

David Del Monté

So when I went into a depression, as I was saying, I asked Jasper that if he was looking for someone to swap with, what about me?

I know that Jasper did not want to swap with me because my life was as boring as his was exciting, but he had trouble finding a subject ever since, after visiting his bedsit installation, fifty students had gone demented after drinking orange juice laced with heliotropic drugs. The two members of Her Majesty's constabulary turned up at the college, but when they heard it was 'the shitting dog,' namely, Jasper, they nodded to each other, readily agreed it was art and made off with a screeching of tyres, glad to avoid the paperwork.

After this, Jasper decided to swap my life, not with his but with that of his old school friend Morgan, who lived in a stately home in Berkshire.

'I can't see anyone pretending to be me for a month if they live in a huge pad, especially if they're going to swap that for my shithole,' I commented, frankly.

'You don't know Morgan,' he said.

When I met Morgan, I still could not believe that a swap would take place. Where his teeth were white and regular, mine were yellow and clustered close together. Where his calves were meaty and fleshed out, his trousers making him a superb clotheshorse, mine were spindly. I had love handles, he was svelte. Later, standing side by side Jasper videoed us. I looked like Morgan's aborted twin, a second, a mistake.

But Morgan, with his sunny face, long nose, bright brown eyes with just a hint of amber, anything was possible.

We found him shooting partridge in his woods and waited patiently while he finished his 'bag,' and then we followed him, picking up some spent cartridges, into the gun room. While he was wiping the guns down and putting them away, Jasper outlined his plan. Morgan slotted a gun into a canvas bag and locked it away in the secure cabinet before bolting and padlocking the door. He wiped his hands on a rag, put his hand on his hip, and rested his weight on a freestanding leg while keeping his other bent at the knee, the boot tip resting on the stone floor.

He sat his butt down on a concrete bench and kicked his legs out so they sprawled in front of him and, with his chin on his chest, allowed his face to take on a slightly more serious expression than his usual boyish demeanour.

'It's a bit much,' he offered, and his voice was plummy and well-fed.

'You have to do it,' Jasper said, 'or I will shoot you.'

Morgan laughed, which I thought was a mistake especially as there was still one gun propped against a wall. 'I suppose you think that would be art!' Morgan cracked, still chuckling.

He was too busy wiping the sweat off his brow with an old canvas rag to notice Jasper slowly nodding.

'You seriously expect me to swap with *him?*' Morgan said. He strode to and fro in the tack room. 'You're nuts.'

'Please, Morgan. It will really mean a lot to me.'

Jasper camped it up something rotten when he wanted to.

'Oh, come on , Jasper, get a grip! You are really childish!'

Jasper went over and whispered something in Morgan's ear. The latter stroked his chin with his long tapering fingers, then rubbed at a black smudge, the start of a bruise made by the recoil of the shotgun into his cheek. Just by accident, the tips of my fingers touched the gun. It was handy to have it nearby in case things went suddenly pear-shaped. With Jasper, you could never be sure.

'Two screws,' he said.

Jasper shook his head.

'No.'

'One screw now and one screw at the end of the month.'

'No,' said Jasper.

'All right then, one screw, all night?'

Jasper nodded.

'OK, but not now. At the end of the month.'

'Done.'

They both shook hands.

Jasper went outside to get Bert, his handler, to unload my stuff as well as the cameras that were to be hidden in the house. Morgan came outside, rubbing his shanks. Then he stretched, like a horse shifting his weight from one hoof to the other.

'OK, let's do it,' he said. 'It can't be as bad as school!'

'Stop chatting and get into his clothes,' Jasper said, holding out a dressing gown for me to change into. 'You need to go now.'

'Is there anything I should know?' asked Morgan, cramming himself into the back of the van and looking suddenly peaky.

'My girlfriend, Sue,' I yelled above the sound of the engine starting. 'She's a sperm junkie.'

Well, I had to say something. Jasper pulled a wry but triumphant expression, grinned, waved a hand, and the van pulled away, driven by Jasper's ever-faithful, the stolid Bert.

In a trice I was wearing Morgan's Burberry shooting kit. I even put on a tie, as all shooters do, over a checked shirt. I had an oilskin to match his hat slung over my arm. I had become Hackett Man.

Meanwhile, Morgan was in my house taking in the 1930s armchairs with their woollen crocheted drapes, the china cabinet, gramophone, and, best of all, the G Plan dining set my grandparents had bought in 1968.

After Morgan was deposited there, my mum made him tea and engaged him in small talk, which tends to have the effect that the manufacturers of the strongest sleeping pills can only dream of. Minutes later Morgan was snoring gently, his head lolled back on the cotton drapes. During this lull Jasper set up hidden video cameras all over the house. He told my mum to call Morgan Ronny (me) and treat him exactly as if he was me. She was not to spare the rod as Morgan was a reformed paedophile, Jasper said. Jasper was his probation officer, he added, and Morgan needed a firm hand.

''E does, does 'e?' said my mum, prodding Morgan awake with a broomstick. She told him to sod off and tidy his room.

'Go on, up with you, you pervert!' which in fact, is how she used to speak to me.

She forced him out into the chilly hall and up the creaky staircase. After he tidied the room as best he could my mum forced him into my narrow bed with its itchy blanket and stained mattress. Later, Morgan was caught on camera wanking on the first night he was there! The only ray of sunshine for him was my PC. He was awoken at 2.00 a.m. by a Skype call from Sue.

'Yah?' he growled after hearing the thing bleat in his ear for a few minutes before he could figure out how to reply.

'Who is this?' Sue demanded.

'Ronny.'

'It doesn't sound like you.'

'Well, that's too bad,' drawled Morgan.

'Oh, OK. Are you naked?'

'As a matter of fact, I am.'

'So am I.'

'Jolly good. The only thing is, I've only just come. Could you call back in the morning?'

She hung up in a hurry and then called again to make sure she could believe her ears.

'Yah?'

'Ronny?'

'Yah.'

'You sound different.'

'Look, I told you, I've already come. Unless you're prepared to drive over here for a good tonguing, I can't do much for you. Good-bye.'

Meanwhile, my mind was full of laughing, dancing characters. Upbeat mood music played continuously in my mind. I was relishing every second of my stay in Morgan's luxuriously appointed state rooms. My mood music grew louder in my ears, especially when Morgan's knockout model girlfriend, Fiona, appeared that very night.

She let herself in with her own key and jumped when she saw me, a tumbler of whiskey in one hand, my feet up on Morgan's living-room sofa, and wearing Morgan's dressing gown.

'Are you a burglar?' she enquired curiously and without any alarm.

'No, I'm not.'

'Well, where's Morgan?'

'He's going to be away for a month. He's in rehab.'

'Rehab? Are you sure?'

'Positive. He's having treatment for homosexual tendencies.'

She stood there looking pale.

'Oh.'

'How recent was your last HIV test?'

'Not very, as a matter of fact.'

'Well, never mind, help yourself to a drink.'

She did as requested, sitting down not far from me, looking like an angel and surrounded by a miasma of some expensive scent that almost made me want to jump her there and then.

Without any prompting, she made a delicious meal with fresh herbs, diced chicken and pasta. Her finesse with the chopping knife boded well for her dexterity in the bedroom, I thought. She had me drinking red wine before taking me upstairs, laughing gaily. She showered and made me do the same. Then we tumbled on to Morgan's magnificent king-sized four-poster bed with its fresh sheets and plumped-up pillows. Having let the towel drop from her perfect body, she got into bed and immediately turned on to her front, revealing her white buttocks. They were as pale as a pair of stones I once found on the beach at Freshwater Bay. But I wasn't sure what to do. She turned on to her back and looked at me out of big eyes like my long-eared rabbit used to do before the fox got it. Her face looked impossibly pale, her teeth impossibly small and white, and her mouth impossibly pink and tender.

'I take it,' she said politely with a cut-glass accent, 'you don't want it up the jacksie?'

'Um? Did you say jacksie?'

'Yes. The jacksie.'

'Is that what Morgan calls it?'

She nodded.

'If it's not too much trouble,' I said, 'I think I'd be happier if we went for the missionary position first.'

She laughed and pushed her hand down to my pecker.

It was as cold and small as a nervous shrimp at Billingsgate Fish Market at 5 a.m. on a winter's morning.

'Shall we see if I can get him to come out to play?' she asked.

And with that she disappeared under Morgan's beautifully laundered sheets. Pretty soon my Johnson, which had not seen active service in aeons, was coming to the boil nicely… and it all went off like a treat.

Poor Morgan, on the other hand, was finding out what it was like to live on the other side of the railway tracks. My mum was merciless. She had him skivvying for her as soon as he woke. There was the bin to empty, the kitchen floor to be washed, the dishwasher to empty, the surfaces to wipe down, the toilets to clean, the carpets to be hoovered, and the front garden to be sorted. That was all in the first hour. Then she demanded he go to Tesco's with the wheelie and bring back groceries. After that, she said, she would give him some man's work to do.

If you wonder why he didn't protest, you don't know my mum. My dad had to have a pacemaker fitted when he was thirty-five. He was invalided out of our house at forty, and died of a heart attack at forty-five, may God have mercy on his soul. My mum took his death as a personal insult. 'If your father could be here now!' she'd say, leaving the words 'I'd give him a piece of my mind' unspoken in the air.

She took easily to calling Morgan 'Ronny,' and I swear by the end of the day she had convinced herself he was me. By five o'clock he was even talking like me.

'Fancy a cuppa?' he asked my mum.

'Go on, then. Now warm the pot, you idle good-for-nothing. Not like that! Do I have to show you everything?'

You couldn't please Mum. Earlier, Morgan who had a fantastic landscaped garden at his estate but who never did any work on it, incurred my mum's wrath when she forced him to tackle our 60 × 20 foot plot at the back of the house.

'I want you to weed, cut the grass, dead-head the roses, and re-pot the geranium,' she insisted.

Poor Morgan! He didn't know one end of a pruning shears from the other. My mum showed him how to do everything but not without beating him around the head with some choice epithets. She could not believe a man was incapable of sorting out a garage, fixing a fuse, mending a washer on a tap, or replacing a lose tile on a roof. 'You play with yourself too much, Ronny. I always told you, you'd go blind.'

'I'm doing my best, Mum,' he'd say, halfway up a ladder, reaching out for the leather tool bag my dad used to own.

'Well your best is crap,' she told him. 'My father…'

And she'd witter on about her amazing dad, a hero in the war, who had hands the size of dinner plates and who could turn water into wine, sell it, make a profit, and build a house on the proceeds.

'What a pity you can't say the same thing about your dad, Ronny.'

'I agree,' said Morgan. 'I never saw my father much after I was eight.'

'How could you? He was dead.'

'You're right, Mum. It's like – he *was* dead!' Morgan said as if my mum were Dr Freud and had sussed the whole thing out.

And so it went on, day after day. He was under her domination from the moment he opened his eyes to the moment he closed them to sleep.

As for me, life went swimmingly. I wore all Morgan's clothes and Fiona even took me to Jermyn Street to buy some more, using a credit card Morgan had given her for her personal use a couple of years before.

I looked – so different. Tailored clothes really do turn a man into a gentleman. And I got into the part. My clothes made people act with respect and deference towards me. People gave way to me in my Range Rover. Policemen even tapped their helmets when they saw me. Traffic wardens sometimes let me off: 'That's all right, guv. I knew you was just loading up!' And a ten pound note by way of thanks did not go amiss anywhere!

I was even invited to Buckingham Palace by a man coming out of White's Club in St James's Street, Mayfair, because he thought I was his grand-nephew!

I received invitations from American Express to attend some private opening, and we went to parties such as you'd never dreamed existed. Although Fiona was ravishing and as Ronny I never would have dreamt of catching a girl anywhere near as fantastic as her, at the parties there were loads of women just like her and they all had the hots for me.

I had a ball! You can imagine, I am sure, what a difference being Morgan made to my life! That, as well as getting away from Mother.

My only anxiety was what was going to happen when the end of the month came around. By the third week, a shadow was hanging over my life. I couldn't even enjoy Fiona's Cordon Bleu cooking .

'Come on,' she'd say, 'try this *Bif a la Provence* The recipe was given to me by Raymond Blanc personally. He is simply divine, darling. We really must go to his Oxford gaff tomorrow ….'

'Fiona, what's going to happen when Morgan comes back? This is all going to come to a sudden and catastrophic end!'

Fiona lifted her finely sculpted head as if she were a gazelle on the African savannah sniffing the spoor of a distant lion.

'Well, there's no point spoiling your digestion. Why don't you finish your meal and we'll talk about it?' she said quietly.

I did so, but I was not my usual self. Fiona played with the hairs on my neck and kissed me, but it was difficult to bring me round. What on earth could be done? The clock was ticking. Afterwards in the drawing room – I should say 'salon,' we were walking through to the library with our drinks, the sound of classical music wafting from room to room as we made our leisurely way to a chaise langue. I said to Fiona that something, surely, could be done.

'Well, darling, I feel just as strongly as you do. But Morgan is the owner of this place, after all. It's been in his family for goodness knows how long – thousands of years I should think, and I am not sure that killing him would do much good. They're bound to know it was you.'

'I'll say it was Jasper! And call it art!'

She shook her head sadly.

'Jasper and Morgan went to the same school. They don't give a toss about anyone and can pull off stunts like that. But you haven't got that kind of steel, poor darling! They'd break you. And they say that prison is terribly boring, you know, especially if you get life. Morgan was in prison once for a drugs bust, but he said it was jolly good fun. But for you it would be awful. I know because a friend of mine was in a Thailand jail for drugs smuggling. But I say, hello? How was she to know? She was just doing that dear sweet oriental man a favour by taking a parcel to his daughter in Brixton. Anyway, she ended up a lesbian. She wasn't really, but she was so bored, you see. She couldn't help herself.'

'It's like a sentence living with her, that's the thing. I think prison might in fact be preferable to going back…'

I nearly said 'to mother,' but I could not bring myself to utter the words.

'You're right,' she said. 'It has been a fairy tale here with you. It wouldn't be the same somewhere else between us, that's true, not even if you left your mother and got a flat or something. There's just something about this place that's special, isn't there?'

I nodded.

'It's got everything a man could want,' I said, putting my hand around Fiona's perfectly shaped bottom.

A few days before the end of the month, Jasper arrived with Bert, in the van, to collect all the cameras from the house. He wasn't looking very pleased. I came out to meet him on the steps.

'What's the matter?' I asked.

'You!' he shouted, jabbing a finger at me.

For a moment I thought he was going to order Bert, who has the physique of a wrestler, to assault me. But I saw that he was too busy videoing me.

'You shit!'

'Oh come on, Jasper. Don't be a prig. Spit it out, old man!' I said.

'You even talk like him. You've been fucking his girlfriend twice daily for a whole month, and you've been plotting to kill him. I've seen all the tapes on my remote! How could you? He's my friend from school, you cunt!'

'Jasper, my dear boy.'

I brought the shotgun out from under my cape.

'Now, why don't you just naff off?'

Jasper looked from my face to the gun and back again.

'Now, come on, Ronny. Don't be a fool. It's got to come to an end some time. You know that. This is for my degree. Don't mess it up, I beg you.'

'I'm Morgan. There is no Ronny,' I said in a deadpan psycho monotone.

'Are you getting this, Bert?' Jasper said as Bert trained a video on me.

'I have proof, you know,' he said.

'Leg it before I shoot the van up,' I ordered, levelling the barrel of the twelve bore in the direction of the vehicle.

'You…!' Screaming an expletive, he leapt into the van.

Fiona came out softly clapping. She'd witnessed the whole thing from the drawing-room windows. Well, they *were* big enough.

'Well, I suppose this is it,' I said to Fiona, glancing at my watch. 'He'll be here any minute.'

She nodded.

'It's been, well, really fun,' she said. 'You're much nicer than Morgan in every way.'

And she tittered and played with my neck the way I liked. We sat in the house and waited, I gloomily, Fiona calmly. She lay with her head in my lap, without moving. I stroked away the strands of her fair hair that sometimes floated across her face, and occasionally I bent down to kiss her pale, pale face that gently warmed to my touch.

We waited all afternoon, but no one came.

We've been waiting ever since.

THE TREATMENT

Years ago, when I travelled on business, I was sometimes lonely. I had not learned the knack, as I have now, of being happy in my own skin. My yearning for human contact used to be so acute that it would drive me into peculiar behaviour, which, I hasten to add, did not venture into committing acts of moral turpitude or illegality. But it is strange and somewhat creepy, I admit, to follow people while remaining unseen by them. And this, I am ashamed to say, is, occasionally, what I did.

One such foray, a walk down the Avenida Paulista in São Paulo in Brazil, led me into a most strange series of events that might scarcely be credible had they not actually taken place.

The Avenida accommodates four lines of traffic, two in each direction. The pavement is crowded too. Most people wear tight-fitting clothes: short sleeves for the men, singlets or skimpy tops for

Coconuts Kill More People Than Sharks

the women. On that day, when the world was ten years younger, I remember a digital display atop a concrete plinth about ten feet high announcing the temperature and the time alternately. It was thirty-one degrees centigrade at 11.20 in the morning.

It was my habit, as I was saying, when I had a few hours to kill, to select a person at random from the mass of people and just follow, unseen, wherever he or she might go. It was just a silly hobby with no nefarious intent.

On that morning my shirt was already clinging to my body like a wet rag. A soft drizzle was falling, which gave everything I saw through my glasses a smeary, translucent effect.

I elected to pound the pavement down one side-street. It did not matter particularly where I went as I was, in any case, entirely lost, or perhaps 'misplaced' would be a better way of putting it. Along this street I found some small shops, little more than openings at the bottom of tall buildings, and there people were standing behind counters stocked with bottles of soda. It was, after all, a warm day and it showed no sign of cooling down. I walked into one of these brightly lit areas. The sign above the shop said FARTO'S. It was a chemist's. A middle-aged woman made a purchase; it was a little plastic hairbrush. She took her item and started to waddle out of the shop. I decided I would follow her, just for something to do. It was funny. She did not walk with purpose. Little things distracted her: shoes in a shop window, an ice-cream vendor, a woman in a white coat asking to buy blood. She zigzagged her way past the stores, stopping at a kiosk to buy a magazine, the top of which later protruded from a small shopping bag she held in the crook of her arm.

Then she set off at a surprisingly brisk pace. I hurried to catch up. We seemed to walk for miles, but perhaps that is because I was tired. My footwear, white gym shoes, didn't help. Eventually, we came to a tall building and entered via a locked gate and a dozing concierge who sat in a box just inside the main doors. I didn't usually enter buildings, but this time I did.

We took an elevator to the twenty-second floor. When the doors opened, we stepped out, and walked past plate-glass windows. I glimpsed the city spreading out over flat land and over small lightly wooded hills and valleys, as far as my eye could see. There were bald patches crammed with shacks with tin roofs, some bald areas filled with one-storey breeze-block dwellings, and even some brown brick houses with swimming pools. Their rectangular pools of blue water looked like little oases in a mass of crammed urbanised humanity. The roofs of corrugated metal were glinting in the sun. My little lady marched briskly off down the corridor and stopped when she came to a door marked CLINIC. She spoke her name into an intercom (it was Magdalena Evian), and we entered when the door gave. A girl in a white uniform, in a white room, greeted us without a smile. She looked like a well-groomed seal, with dark hair parted down the middle. She frowned as she studied the computer screen, then looked up.

'What is it you want, Magdalena?' she asked in Portuguese.

'I want the treatment.'

Lights popped on inside the girl's eyes like minute torch beams.

'I told you when you came in yesterday: you can't have the treatment, there is a waiting list.'

'I need it. It's not fair.'

'It all goes by birth date. And other factors I am not at liberty to disclose.'

The torch beams went out, and the pupils of her eyes widened into black pools as she settled on me.

'Name?' she asked in a metallic tone.

I gave it. She punched some keys on the computer.

'Does it say how long I have to wait?' Mrs Evian asked.

'No. You just have to be patient.'

Her lips moved as she read something off the screen.

'James Riley. You can come next week. We have one slot available. Can you make it?'

'Is he having the treatment? How come he can get an appointment, and not me?' Mrs Evian demanded.

'You can have mine,' I offered.

'Appointments are not transferable.'

'Why not?' Mrs Evian asked.

'Listen lady, I don't make the rules. I can't go against the programme. Kindly step aside and let me deal with this gentleman. Is 3.00 p.m. on Thursday OK for you?'

'For the treatment?' I said.

'For the treatment.'

I had no idea how my name ended up on her database, or whether I was the same James Riley who was entitled to an appointment.

She sighed, and printed out a small appointment slip.

'Your Portuguese is very good. *Bom dia*.'

I should have asked and got the whole thing sorted out there and then, but everything happened so fast. Moreover, it was against my rules to interact with a subject like this. The whole point of the game was to remain undetected and merely to study the subject's movements and glean what one could about their lives without their being aware of one's presence.

When I got back to my hotel I asked my friendly concierge what he knew about the treatment.

'Don't tell me you don't know what it is, Mr James!' he said.

His scornful remark dissuaded me from enquiring further.

So I showed up at the appointed hour.

A doctor came and sat with me.

'Are you completely in the picture? Do you know what is involved? There will be no time for regrets afterwards.'

He pushed a sheaf of what looked like disclaimer papers for me to sign.

'Doctor, I wonder, could you just enlighten me a little as to what is going to happen?'

'To your body, you mean?'

'Well – yes.'

'You are a very lucky individual. There are millions queuing up for this treatment.'

'Which is?'

'The treatment?'

'Yes.'

'Well, where do I start? Let us list the benefits: perpetual happiness for a start; no headaches, total absence of pain, and what is more, no ageing and no more limits on space and time.'

'Doctor, can you run that last one by me again, the one about escaping limits on space and time?'

'Exactly right. You didn't hear about Sting's voyage to the outer galaxy?'

'I don't think so.'

'Light travels at 300,000 miles a second. Think of the places you'll see....'

'Thanks, doctor, but I don't think…'

'It's only an injection, that's all. There is nothing to be afraid of.'

He gripped me firmly by the wrist and then let me go.

'I'm sorry. Would you like some time to think about it?'

'I've just never met anyone who's had it done.'

'You should have told me. You need to meet Jamila, our receptionist.'

He was referring to the contented seal at the front desk.

'She was HIV free, of course. And now she continues to live a pure life. The treatment is painless and guaranteed. Do you wish to proceed?'

'Is there a cost?'

The doctor laughed the kind of laugh typical of kids when you find they have hidden a shoe you want to put on. A lot was being lost in translation here; I just could not get a straight answer to a straight question. What was going to happen to me? I don't know what, but it must be a result of my fogged up state of mind, my lack of clarity caused by my loneliness at the time, that led me to go along with the whole thing.

'Of course there is a charge, my friend! Isn't there a charge for everything? But you have a credit card, no?'

I did but I needed to know the price.

At that moment, Jamila sashayed into the room, fireworks sparking in her eyes.

'James Riley, you are getting a 70 per cent discount because you came in with Mrs Evian!'

That said, the fireworks went out and were replaced by the usual placid dark pools. I handed over my credit card. She took it away and came back grinning a few minutes later. Now the doctor took over, waving her away as she returned my card. We both watched Jamila from the rear as she wiggled her way back the way she had come.

'You will have one injection and wake up, completely normal. The change will be undetectable for a long time to come. And then, you will see… why the treatment is so popular.'

He told me to make a closer inspection of Jamila who did indeed look healthy and well. She smiled, pouted, stood up, and swivelled her hips like a dancer to demonstrate her svelte figure and all-over glow. I had to admit she looked pretty good. But then, maybe she had always looked like that.

Inside a small room, strapped to a chair, I had the injection.

The next thing I knew I was awake in my pyjamas in my hotel bed in São Paulo.

I felt great. My head felt heavy as if I had been out all night, but mentally I felt alive and tingling. I got out of bed, had a bath, and put on my clothes. A numbness such as you get after a long sleep, in which every limb that has spent the previous eight hours immobile started to dissipate, as I moved about, swinging my arms and skipping on my feet to get my circulation going. In fact, I felt great, self-contained, and liberated from the previous day's grip of loneliness.

Well, this was an improvement, undoubtedly! No wonder Magdalena Evian had so desired this treatment! I was happy to recommend it to anyone, to judge from my new-found vitality.

It did indeed prove to be the case. I zoomed about town doing my appointments and then later, having time on my hands, followed sundry people. It was a habit hard to break, I guess. One, a young woman in black trousers and a white singlet top, walked for ages, and I ended up beating her down to her high-rise abode. I watched outside as she entered her apartment, switched on the light (it was night by now), and settled down to watch TV. I saw her boyfriend or husband arrive, and I saw them argue, gesticulating, until the girl walked into another room plunging the living room and kitchen into darkness.

At that point I decided to give up this silly pastime and return to my hotel. I simply did not need to do such crazy things any more. The next few days passed quickly as, with ever-increasing energy and brio, I completed all my commercial transactions successfully and returned home to the UK.

Immediately upon my return, my wife remarked on how good I looked, except for my eyes.

'They look rather odd. Have you been overdoing it, my love?' she asked.

I looked in the mirror. My face looked good, the flesh tighter and more defined, but the eyes did seem a little more deep-set than before and, perhaps, a little red on the lower lids, betokening fatigue. Of course my wife did not know of my following expeditions, and clearly, as they did not reflect well on my character, I kept knowledge of them from her.

The only other change in me was a reduced libido. My wife did not mind too much. We slept in the same bed, but we did not make love more than once a month. I found I had no desire for her at all. Nor had I much appetite, despite the fact that I still woke up brimful of energy.

Then, one Saturday morning as I was trying to hang a picture on the wall, I hammered a nail into my thumb, instead of into the wall. I experienced a jolt of pain, but when I withdrew the nail no blood emerged from the entry point. Indeed, I watched as the tiny circular hole closed completely, leaving no mark at all. I resolved to go to the doctor the next morning and get myself checked over.

I had no appointment but was lucky to find my regular doctor present at 8.30 a.m. and he agreed to give me a look-over. He soon had me coughing, sticking out my tongue, and so on. He got me to remove my shirt and vest, ran a stethoscope over my chest, looked in my ears and my eyes, and sat down, drumming a pencil against his teeth.

'What do you think, doctor? Do I need a blood test?'

The pencil drumming ceased and he looked at me quizzically.

'Let me be the judge of that,' he said cryptically. 'Where did you say you had the treatment done?'

'Brazil.'

'Ah-ha.'

He was being opaque, as only doctors can.

'Did anyone mention any side effects?' he asked.

'No – not really.'

'Well then, perhaps the time has come for me to tell you what they are.'

'OK.'

I sat in the chair and listened. The doctor kept large photographs of his two sons in the consulting room, caught at various stages of their development. One was tall, the other short. Slowly, as they grew to adulthood, their respective sizes decreased so that they ended up more or less the same height. Four photographs charted this development, from shy boys in their bar mitzvah suits, to young men in desert fatigues, arms around each other, rifles slung over shoulders. I studied these as the doctor wittered on, but there was nothing in his description that fitted my symptoms.

'Your white blood count is likely to be high,' he said. 'And that is probably why no blood emerged when you hurt your thumb with the nail. Of course, as you must know, in the end you won't need any white blood cells at all.'

What did he mean by 'in the end'?

'You see,' the doctor began, 'The point is... how can I put this... you have undergone a procedure that involves irreversible cell replacement.'

'What does that mean?' I asked.

'Well, put in simple layman's terms,' the doctor said, 'we are all, as you know, concerned with our carbon footprint.'

'Of course,' I said, genuflecting respectfully to this sound doctrine. 'Our carbon footprint is highly relevant.'

'Indeed. We have received a report from the government with a lot of very practical recommendations for reducing our carbon footprint.'

'Oh yes?' I asked.

'Yes indeed. And of course one way is via means of the treatment you yourself have been so lucky to procure.'

'Oh, good,' I said.

'The human being,' the doctor went on, twiddling the pencil between his thumbs and leaning back in his chair, 'Is an exceptionally greedy creature, demanding of ever more finite resources. Your treatment, luckily, reverses that trend. It is estimated that if 99 per cent of the population has the same treatment as you have had, the carbon footprint will be reduced by the same amount.'

'That is astonishing,' I said, 'And no doubt very pleasing to the government.'

'Oh yes, it certainly is! In fact, the treatment will soon appear as a United Nations policy for best practise and, following the eighth protocol of the Geneva Convention and backed up by the Kyoto Agreement and its successors, every country in the world will need to put in place a similar treatment programme as has been pioneered in overcrowded countries such as Brazil, with help from the World Bank.'

I jibbed a little at his depiction of Brazil as overcrowded as it was, of course, nothing of the kind. São Paulo is, to be sure, a forty square mile plus conurbation of forty million or so citizens, but the rest of the country is relatively lightly settled.

'I myself,' he went on, 'have been serving on the committee for the introduction of the treatment into this country. And has the effect on you been beneficial?'

I had to agree that overall, it had been. My mood swings had decreased, I was full of energy and what was more, I did not really care much about anyone around me. I mean, that I maintained a mood of equanimity in all circumstances, rather akin to the Buddhist notion of detached goodwill.

I wore a perpetually amiable smile and although I enjoyed seeing my wife and family about their business watching TV, eating, or playing games, it mattered not a lot to me whether they were there or not. I was happy wherever I was, and my mood did not change, not even when it rained or when the sun was out.

'All in all,' said the doctor, 'I do not think you have anything to worry about. The loss of libido you mentioned – is that a bad thing? I mean, look at the energy you save by not making love. There is the saving on water, since you naturally have to wash before and after sex. And remember that sex at your age and your already having kids, is really a luxury. It is merely a gratification of the hormonal urges within you, which itself is quite wasteful, when you think about it.'

I agreed that, put like that, he was correct. What was the point of such exercise, really? Might it be better to workout instead? Or go for a run?

'Granted,' he said, 'up until now exercise has been recommended. But consider the extra food you will consume after exercise. As you remarked, you have a reduced appetite. That can only be good, as it reduces the carbon footprint still further.'

'And will I remain in this happy state for ever, or will the effects wear off?'

'I believe those who have had the treatment will always benefit from it. I myself will be undergoing the procedure in the next few days, as will most of my patients. An exciting future awaits us,' he said, putting the pencil down and smiling.

'In the end, my boy,' he went on, really warmed up to his theme, 'There will be no more suffering in the world and no more children either.'

'No more children?' I asked.

'They won't be necessary. They are far too expensive to rear, and in the future there will be no more need for them. Think of the money that will be saved by cutting the child benefit that is paid in billions every year!'

'Well, how will the human race continue?' I asked.

'It won't. In our new form we will be able to voyage to other galaxies, or indeed, venture nowhere at all.'

'How will we be able to do that?'

'Well, I am not sure how it will work out in the practical sense,' he admitted. 'But in theory such voyages will be possible.'

I mentioned Sting.

'Well exactly. Perhaps Mr Sting has made such a voyage and perhaps he has not,' the doctor went on, 'but theoretically it is possible.'

Still, I pondered, a world without children was a little drastic.

I needed further explanation. But now the doctor's time had run out.

He clapped me on the back and shook my hand.

'I wish you every success in your life,' he said, his eyes twinkling. 'Well done for being such a pioneer!'

I asked him, while he held the door open for me, whether I should have a blood test just to be on the safe side.

'There's no need. Soon, you will have no blood.'

'No blood?'

'That is correct. Your carbon footprint will be zero. You will soon exchange human tissue and organs for, well, for want of a better word, light.'

'Light?'

'Well, you see, light is a wonderful substance. It requires very little energy to sustain itself. In a way, it is energy. Your body, being made of bones, blood, skin, and so on requires a heavy injection of valuable food stocks. But light requires very little. Just a spot of sun, really.'

'What about my brain, my mental processes?'

'You won't need any. It would be possible to encase your mind inside a SIM card the size of a pinhead. But then you would not be able to travel through space-time. Liberated from all organic matter you will soon be able to travel through the universe at the speed of light, which as you know is…'

'Three hundred thousand miles per second.'

'Correct. So, as you can see, a really bright future awaits us all.'

'Just one last point, doctor,' I said.

'Yes, what is it?' he asked glancing at his watch, a little too rudely for my liking. 'I do have one or two other patients…'

'What if someone turns off the light?'

He arched his eyebrows at this idea.

'I suppose such an action might be possible in the future. And then we would all cease to be. But there would be no carbon footprint by then.'

'Except that of the person turning the switch,' I said.

'Exactly,' he agreed with a ready smile, his cheeks flushed with blood. 'And think how lonely that person will be, left on his own. He would be the only bit of organic matter left on the Earth.'

'Yes, I suppose it would be rather lonely,' I agreed. 'Perhaps such a person, becoming light themselves eventually, would be destined to hunt in the galaxy for other like-minded individuals. It would be a lonely, fruitless quest through space-time, lasting centuries, even aeons, travelling at the speed of light.'

'Yes,' said the doctor wistfully, gazing over the heads of his stirring, restless patients into the middle of the distant wall above their heads. 'Wouldn't that be truly extraordinary?'

I agreed that it would, and departed the medical practise, buttoning up my overcoat against the chilly wind that, within a few short months, I was destined not to feel.

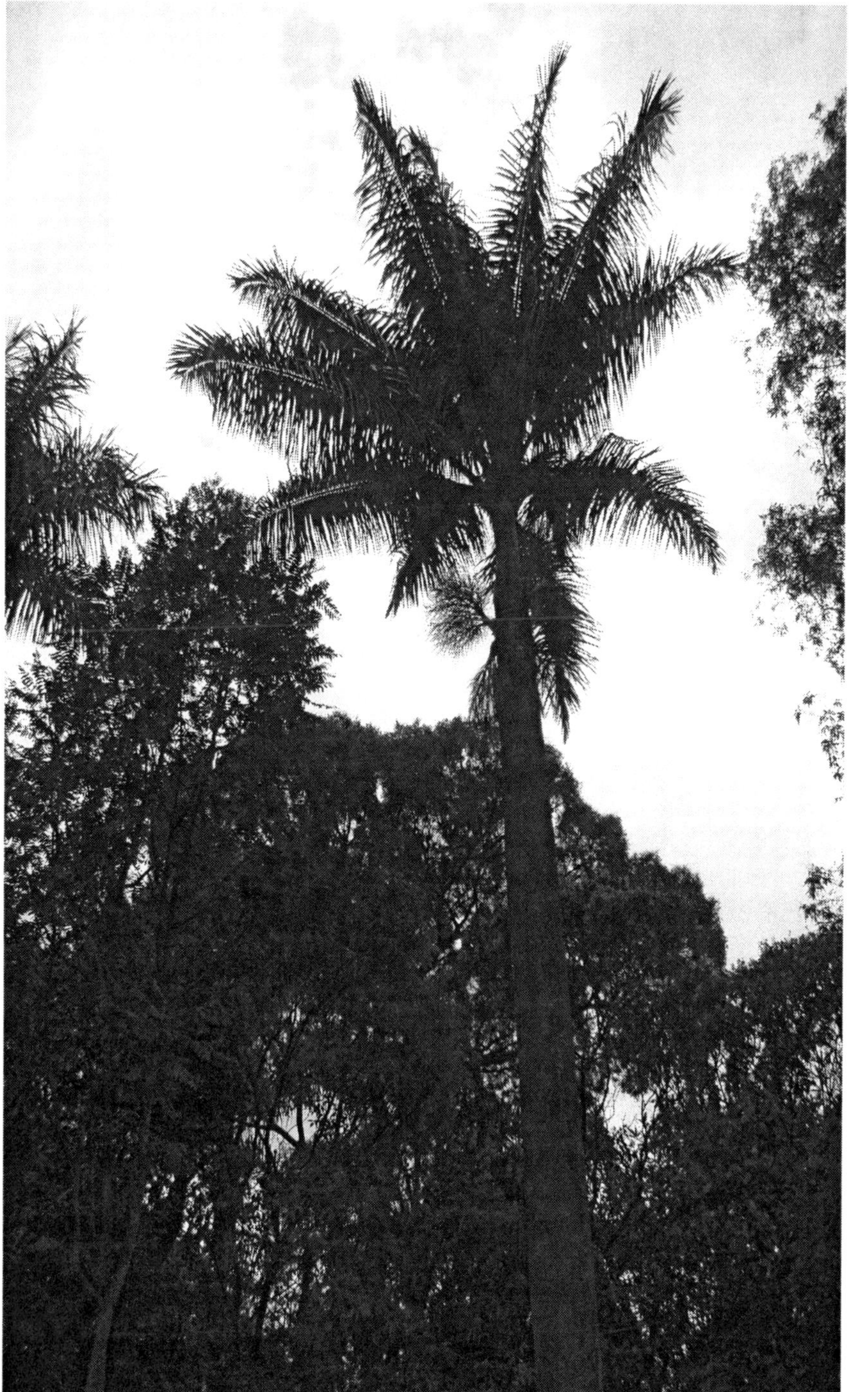

COCONUTS KILL MORE PEOPLE THAN SHARKS

On 15 December 2004, Mr and Mrs Brown from Colchester were sitting outdoors having breakfast at the Hotel Sunvalley in the Dominican Republic, when at 8.21 a.m., a coconut fell from the heavily laden palm tree above and killed Mr Brown instantly. Mrs Brown sued her tour company, Funtours, claiming that the couple should have been warned beforehand of the danger that a palm tree might pose and that the hotel and/or the travel company were negligent in seating them under one.

The company argued that a falling coconut was an act of God that it could not reasonably have predicted. Mrs Brown's counsel argued that to sit customers in an area where they might be subjected to falling objects the size of rugby balls was foolhardy, and the tour company should not have allowed it to happen. Mrs Brown was suing not for her husband's future earnings, as he was already retired, but for the loss of companionship and the emotional 'deletion' that she would suffer as a consequence of having to holiday alone in future. She also claimed for the distress caused by witnessing the incident.

On the fourth day of the trial, Funtours Head of Health and Safety, Peter Benson, took the witness stand.

He was a slightly built man with a straggly comb-over and spectacles. He sported a tweed jacket baggy at the elbows and made a striking contrast to the slick lawyer acting for the plaintiff, Hector Streicher, who, licking his lips and grinning, seemed sure of demolishing his prey.

Streicher began calmly enough.

'How long have you worked for your employers?'

'Funtours? Seventeen years.'

'And you have been Head of Health and Safety for let me see, five years.'

Benson nodded.

'Can you answer the question,' interpolated the judge. 'For the record.'

'Oh yes. He's right. I mean, that is correct. I've worked there for five years.'

Streicher grinned. Round One in the bag: he had unsettled the witness.

'I suppose you have dealt with many accidents.'

'Oh yes!'

'And you have, I understand, been responsible for drawing up advice for reps to hand out, or explain, to customers?'

'That is correct, yes.'

'Could you give the Court some examples?'

Benson's body jerked in a kind of spasm. He looked across at his counsel's table but no help was coming from that quarter. Impassive or mildly curious faces met his anxious mien from each quarter of the room. He was on his own.

'For example,' boomed Streicher in a kindly tone, 'you carry out risk assessments, I take it?'

'Oh yes. I do.'

'Can you give us some examples?'

'I hope this is leading somewhere,' commented the Judge,

'I assure Your Honour, it is,' assured Streicher.

'Well, my advice has to be comprehensive. I have to try to imagine any evantuality that might befall a pax.'

'Pax?'

'Sorry, that is travel agent speak for customer. Basically, I warn and gather data on any kind of incident that might or could cause injury to pa- I mean customers.'

'For example?' pressed Streicher.

'For example, we warn people not to look up at the sun with the naked eye. Or walk through glass doors when they are closed.'

'I fear you are being too modest,' said Streicher, drawing himself up to his not inconsiderable height. 'I have here some of the health and safety advice that you routinely give to clients. I quote: Brazil is a hot country. It has nuts. If you decide to eat them, do not attempt to crush them yourself using your hands, fingers, knees, or teeth. Do not insert them in door jambs or attempt to smash them using glass ashtrays. Please use the nutcrackers provided by the hotel. If you find that the nut does not break, it is probably because it is a stone. Do not eat stones. Do you recognize the authorship of these words?'

Benson nodded. 'Yes, I wrote them.'

'Are you not being a little over anxious here?'

'Oh no, not at all. I have also had cases of people touching electricity cables while walking outside their resorts and, and getting electrocuted.'

'What did you advise after that?'

'Not to go outside of their resorts.'

'Did that solve the problem?'

Benson shook his head, warming now to themes with which he was intensely familiar.

'People still fall off their jeeps during safaris, drown in pools, slip on wet floors…and so on.'

'I see. Did you write the following? In the case of a death of a passenger while in mid-flight, the toilet may be used to store the corpse whilst in transit. If the toilet is occupied and a corpse remains in his or her seat, it will be the responsibility of the live passenger sitting next to him or her to ensure that his or her seat belt is fastened, their tray table has been put away, and the seat back of their chair is in the upright position prior to landing. '

Streicher finished reading and the judge admonished the public gallery for laughing.

'I take it you find nothing amusing about writing such advice?' Streicher asked.

'None whatsoever.'

'I have several examples that an objective person might view as showing signs of levity.'

'Not at all.'

'Well, may I quote you another example of your advice? Better still, why don't you read it out to the Court?'

Streicher held out a typewritten piece of paper and the sergeant at arms handed it up to the witness. Benson took the flapping page in his hand, and read silently.

'Aloud if you do not mind!' admonished Streicher.

Benson started tentatively enough, but gained confidence as he read.

'It is best to ignore beggars and children who are not your own. If you want to ignore your own children for the duration of your holiday, our mini-club staff is available. They can be identified by their blue and canary yellow uniforms. They will never ask for money. If they do, they are kidnappers and do not work for the hotel. '

'And you are not telling me you did not write this tongue in cheek?'

'No, I did not!' said Benson hotly.

At this point, Streicher, realizing that his victim was primed and lulled into a false sense of security now asked in a genial voice:

'What about sharks?'

Benson, his cheeks already warm with emotion, was relieved to be on safer ground. He began to speak and to show off a little, displaying his mastery of detail.

'We have reams of advice on how to deal with sharks! We tell people to always stay in groups, not to wander too far from shore, to avoid being in the water during darkness or twilight hours when sharks are most active. Not to enter the water if bleeding from an open wound or if menstruating, not to wear shiny jewellery because the reflected light resembles the sheen of fish scales....'

'So you are telling the Court that your advice on sharks is pretty comprehensive?'

'Absolutely.'

'Then why, pray,' announced Steicher in a loud voice, 'do you have no information at all about the dangers of coconuts?'

A hush fell upon the Court. Benson stood there dumbstruck.

'Coconuts?' he asked.

'I mean,' said Streicher, 'you give a warning, as we have heard, in case a person bites on a stone instead of a nut. In case someone touches a live electric cable. Or slips up. Or...'

'Or runs out of condoms, ' said Benson helpfully.

'But coconuts....?'

He let his arms flap out and back like a penguin. Without perhaps realizing it Benson mimicked him in the same way that Manuel does in *Fawlty Towers*.

'Is the reason for this because you imagine that coconuts do not pose a danger to your pax?'

'There's b-been no data,' stammered Benson.

'Indeed, is that a fact?' asked Streicher, relishing his moment of triumph.

'Isn't it true that, according to George Burgess, Director of the University of Florida's International Shark Attack File, falling coconuts kill 150 people worldwide each year? 15 times the number of fatalities attributable to sharks?'

'I have heard of this claim, 'said Benson, 'but I have never heard of anyone being bitten on the leg by a coconut.'

Benson chuckled at his witticism but as he looked around the court, he realized he was the only one.

'This is no laughing matter. A man has died, a customer of your employers,' said the Judge with some anger in his voice.

'Of course, My Lord. I meant no offence,' replied Benson.

'150 people per year die of coconuts falling on their heads. 15 times more than die from shark attack,' Streicher went on, 'yet not one word in your 1500 pages of Health and Safety advice. Instead we read the following under the subject of obesity. 'Our airplane seats are an industry-standard 28 inches. For those passengers who cannot fit into our seats comfortably, an extra charge will be made for the second buttock. ' Is Health and Safety a joke to you, Mr Benson?'

'No,' said Benson quietly, 'it is just company policy.'

Shortly after the judge's somewhat scathing summing up, the jury retired and after only half an hour brought in a decision for the Plaintiff.

'Damages for the Plaintiff set at $55 million,' said the Judge,

Counsel for the defendant stood and lodged an appeal. It never happened because two days later Benson was fired from his job and Funtours went into bankruptcy. Mrs Brown never got a single cent of compensation. And Benson, sitting on a Caribbean beach, having retired from all daytime activity, was wont to look up at the coconut trees and formulate health and safety policy in his head. It was true, he had not written one word of advice about avoiding falling coconuts. Even though he had wracked his brain about everything else he could think of, the dangers of falling coconuts had escaped him completely. What could he have advised? Pax to wear hard hats while eating their breakfasts? Castrating every palm tree in sight? It did not much matter because he was unemployed. But gathering up the bunch of necklaces with which he made his $20 dollar per week meagre living, he did not care. With only shorts and a pair of flip-flops to support, he did not need any health and safety advice at all. He just made sure he kept away from trees.

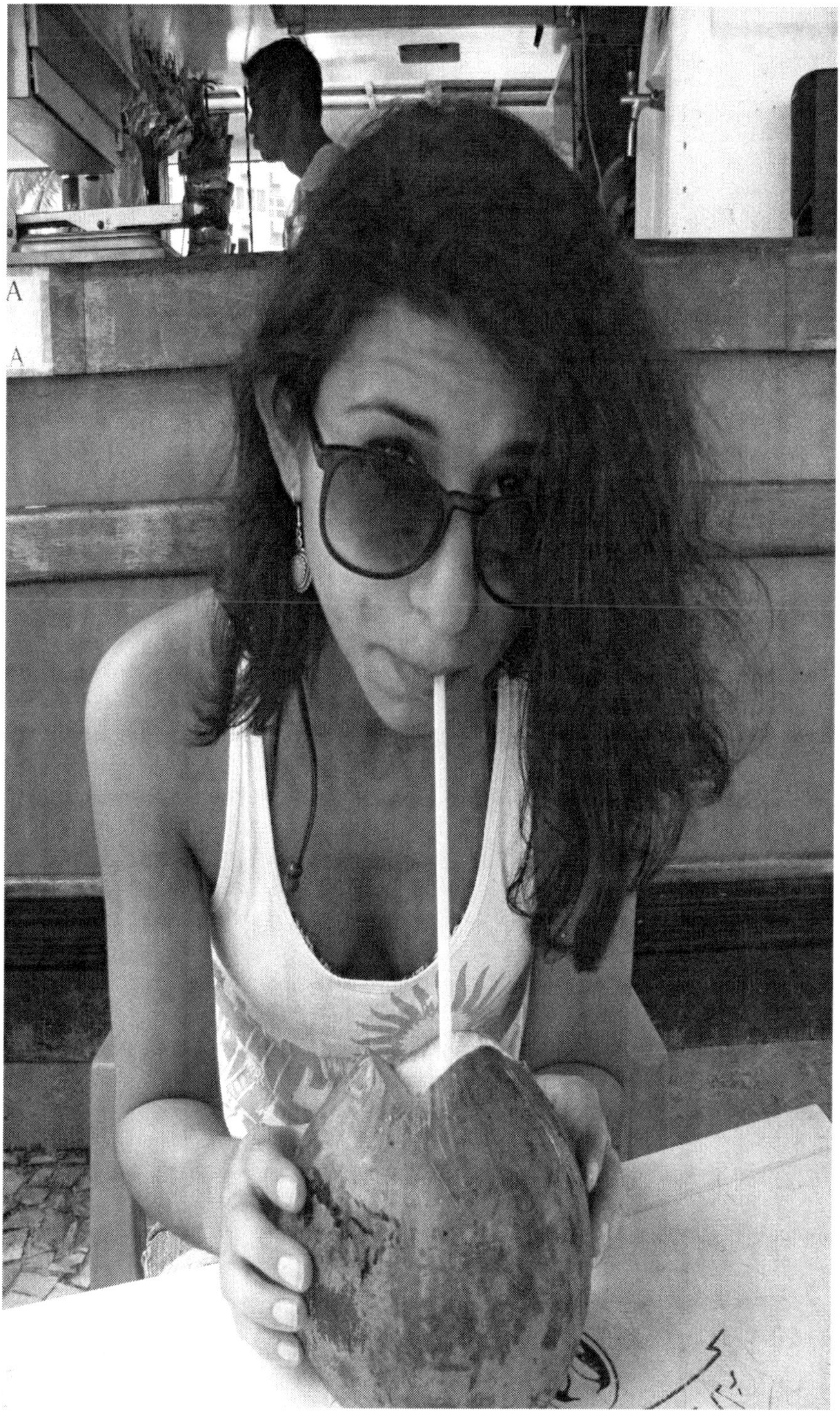

QUANTUCK LUBECK'S INHERITANCE

Quantuck Lubeck's last job before leaving the cobbled high street of his hometown, was to visit the three single-storey stone buildings his father had left him and dispose of them. This was easier said than done because Quantuck had been brought up in another town by his mother and had never seen the buildings before. Not knowing his father at all, Quantuck expected to find the assets broken down and worthless. To his surprise the first had been converted into a pub, and, to judge by the splendid coat of arms swinging from the iron work, it did a thriving trade. He might as well sell the leasehold to the publican. The next building was a library – at least according to the paper sign in the window. And the third – Quantuck never got to see the third. He stopped at the second. This building, identical to the first, was built in the gothic style and stood, like its partner, in a prominent place in the centre of an open area of the town.

Quantuck was intrigued. What would his father, whom he knew to be a hard-headed man of business, want with a library? He knocked on a small blue door at the side. A slim girl dressed in a simple skirt and white woollen top opened the door.

'Yes?'

'I am Quantuck Lubeck, the owner.'

It was best to be direct, he decided.

She looked down, then up and invited him in, retreating and turning sideways to allow him to pass her in the narrow passageway. This led to the main accommodation. The building was, in fact, only one long room. Rafters held the roof in place, and he could see immediately that 'the library' contained no books, no, not even shelves. Lubeck confronted an empty room.

'What are you doing here?' he asked.

She shifted uneasily before him, and shuffled her shoes on the dusty linoleum.

'Well, are you the cleaner?'

She shook her head.

'Your father…' she began.

'Yes,' Quantuck said impatiently, 'my father, what about my father?'

'He says you're to take me with you.'

He stared at her. She would not raise her head to him. Two curtains of bob-length dark hair almost completely obliterated her face.

'I'm to take you with me?' he echoed. 'And where to, might I ask?'

Now she looked up at him.

'America.' she said, her face bright. 'Take me with you to America.'

'Why? Don't you like it here?'

She looked uncomfortable; tussling, it seemed, with doubts and ideas she could not put into words. It was bad not to love your own country, of course it was, and she did not want to be unpatriotic. She looked up at him.

'Your father said our people need a strong leader who will stand on their heads. If no one stands on our heads we will kill each other. Now he is dead. Everything will again…' irritatingly for Quantuck, she tailed off.

'Again what? What are you talking about, stand on people's heads?' he said loudly.

'They will start killing each other! They have hatred in their hearts. But your father stood on their heads. He kept them down. They could not fight. Now they are free. They see themselves as different people, different nationalities.'

'I see,' he said hurriedly, to cut off her flow. 'And what of this, this library?'

'This is the library of understanding,' she said, almost reverently, looking about the empty area.

'But there are no books,' he said.

'You don't understand,' she said. 'This is for you. When you come back from America a rich man, you will make a foundation here. For understanding. That was your father's wish.'

'And where do you fit into all this?' he asked, looking for a chair to sit down upon and finding only a packing case. He jumped up on to this, and gesturing, offered her the other side, which she declined, shaking her head.

'I am to be your guide, your muse, your helpmeet, your talisman, your reminder to come home, and…'

'And what?'

She blushed a little.

'Your woman.'

He sat on the packing case and looked at her again. What was she? One of his father's mistresses?

'Shall we go to the pub and talk about it?' he suggested.

'No,' she said. 'No one must know of this.'

'How old are you?' he asked, suddenly suspicious.

'Thirteen,' she said.

'Do your parents know about your plan?'

She shook her head.

'Did my father?'

She shook her head.

Then Quantuck acted uncharacteristically. He slipped off the packing case, stepped forward, grasped the girl by her slender shoulders, and kissed her lightly on the face. It was a nice face. And her teeth, like the rest of her, were pristine, too young really, for him or for anyone.

'We'll take the night train tonight,' he told her, 'to Paris.' He felt her squirm with pleasure in his arms.

'You'll be Mrs Lubeck,' he told her, and although he could not see her face beneath her bob which hung down on both sides of her face, he knew she was smiling.

Many years later, when they had children, and Lubeck had become, as she had predicted, a rich man, she asked him why he had chosen her.

'Poetry,' he said. 'You had poetry.'

That made her hug his arm even harder.

'Besides,' he said, 'you were right.'

They surveyed the ruined centre of their old town. The three buildings were roofless and burnt out.

'And for what?' he asked.

'Come,' said Mrs Lubeck, 'let's go home.'

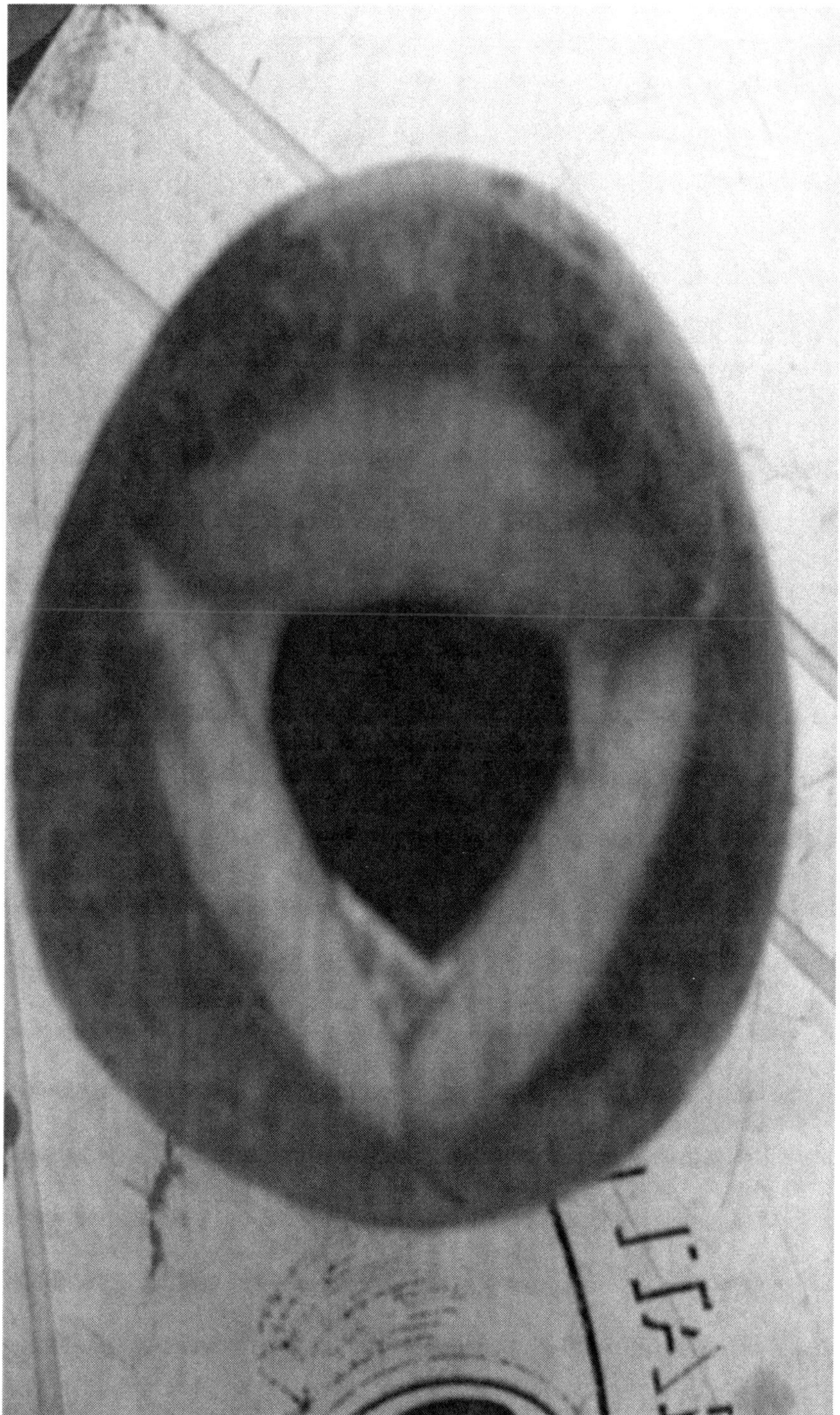

A DREAM OF WILSON PICKETT'S

Usually, Wilson Pickett didn't have dreams. He slept for around eight hours every night and viewed this time (if he thought about it at all) as a period set aside solely for R and R (rest and recovery). If he did have a dream, he could never recollect it. Some time last week (there is no need to be exact in the matter), for some unaccountable reason, Wilson couldn't switch off. His wife subsided into her habitual dormancy, punctuated by laborious and loud breathing as soon as her head hit the pillow. Wilson lay beside her, his mind unusually excited, although, for the life of him, Wilson knew he had nothing on earth to be excited about. He tried everything. He went downstairs and watched an old Western on TV. He went so far as to pour himself a finger of cognac his wife kept for cooking purposes. Finally, at around 4.00 a.m., he went upstairs, threw himself on to the bed with a grunt, and passed, erratically, into a kind of sleep. In the morning he woke and went to work with a dead head. That night he went to bed at the unseasonable hour of eight o'clock and slept twelve hours. Just before he woke, however, Wilson had a dream. The dream, briefly, was this.

Wilson sat in his car in a supermarket car park, one of those with concrete pillars, a low ceiling, and neon lights. While sitting there, in his 'car-coon' minding his own business, he saw a woman walk by. She was absolutely naked, except for a pair of white knee-high boots. Although there were plenty of shoppers around, no one except Wilson seemed to pay her any mind. He noted the fact that her pubic area was entirely hairless, and on her neatly rounded breasts, her nipples were faintly discernible as small brown dots. The woman walked to her own car and sat down inside. Wilson got out of his car and, without hesitation, strode over. He stood by the open car window.

'I couldn't help noticing,' he said, 'that you're not wearing any clothes.'

'Yes, that is for health reasons,' the woman replied calmly.

'To get air around your body, you mean?' Wilson said, with a straight face.

'Yes.'

Although her body was slender and youthful, the skin around her throat was coarse and loose. She had dark hair that hung around her shoulders. Her face was pleasant enough. Wilson, engorged with desire, struggled to keep the conversation on an even keel.

'Is this a hobby of yours? Do you regularly go around like this?'

'Only on doctor's orders,' the woman replied. 'But I'm quite happy to be invited out.'

With a typically adroit style, Wilson moved in for the kill.

'Would you care, for example, to come out to the theatre?' he asked.

'I'd like that very much,' she said, 'Provided, it is at a time when my husband isn't around.'

The fact that he'd have to lie to his wife in order to go out with another woman hit Wilson like a slap in the face. Unaware of his anxieties, the woman passed a small piece of paper, on which she had written a telephone number, through the window. Then, with a smile, she drove off.

It was at this point that Wilson woke up. He played the dream over in his mind, trying hard to remember all its salient parts, and as he got out of bed he found himself reaching for a piece of paper on his desk and a biro, and writing down a number which came to his mind unbidden. He crumpled the piece of A4 in his hand and shoved it into his trouser pocket. Without washing (because he was running a little late), he dressed and went downstairs for breakfast. As soon as he got to work, he dialled the number.

'Yes?' A woman's voice answered.

'My name is Wilson Pickett. I'm sorry to call you….'

'That's OK,' replied the female voice. It had the same calm quality as the one in his dream. 'I was wondering when you would.'

Now there was a pause while Wilson scrambled to think what to say.

'I'm free most evenings,' the voice continued.

'Good. Perhaps you'd like to meet me at the theatre?'

'Great! Could we do a pre-dinner?'

'Certainly.'

He suggested a popular Thai restaurant in Rupert Street, London W1. The woman agreed and the conversation ended. He had arranged for the meeting to take place the following evening. He told his wife he was going to meet an old male school friend, whom he knew was out of town that day. He sloped off as soon as he could after work, and, wearing his best get-up, a suit with a bright fancy waistcoat, he loitered outside the restaurant. On the dot of 6.45, the appointed time, the woman approached. He couldn't mistake her. She came walking towards him from the top of Rupert Street, which is on a slight incline. She wore the same knee-high white boots. And she was stark naked. No one seemed to pay her any mind. They went inside and sat down. Wilson imagined that some objection might be made by the restaurant management, but there not a bit of it. The woman complied with all the conventions, taking a menu and sitting upright while she read it.

'What do you fancy eating?' asked Wilson.

'Well, I'm vegetarian,' the woman said, her head still buried in the menu.

'Really?'

'I trust you are, too.'

'Me? No. I don't eat much meat. The odd chicken…'

'Chicken? Don't you realise the chicken you kill has the right to come back and kill you in a future life?'

This put a damper on the conversation. A waiter sidled up and asked them what they wanted to drink. But Wilson didn't order. He went to the bathroom. He stood there looking at himself in the mirror. Youthful desires still occupied his thoughts, but he was looking at an older face. The skin on his throat wobbled. Now he was beginning to feel seriously disorientated. He didn't know who this woman was. He didn't know what was going on. How could he conduct himself with her? What was he getting into? What was more, he had bought two expensive tickets to see *Edward III* at the Gielgud Theatre. He wanted to see the play, but with this woman? He had no idea as to her provenance. And by the sound of her she appeared to be a real harpy. Still, he didn't have much option but to go through with the ordeal. Perhaps the play would turn out all right. He washed his hands under the hot tap, dried them, and went out to the table.

After the meal, they trooped up the street without a word. The play was good and at the end of it the woman bade him farewell on the busy pavement outside the theatre, and disappeared into the night.

Back home, his wife asked him how he had spent his evening. He didn't appreciate the precision of the question. Some elision if not outright evasion, was required. The best tactic was to keep it all vague. He looked at her pear-shaped body without emotion.

'The evening went OK,' he told her.

Later she got changed into her nightie, and lay down beside him. As soon as he got to bed he found he couldn't sleep. Neither could his wife. She rolled towards him and wafted garlic breath in his direction. This was the woman he'd lived with for twenty years. He could not say he was disappointed. Her behaviour was predictable to a point, but she was congenitally good humoured and easy to please. She was not often tense, and she loved the small terraced house and garden. No, he could not say he lacked for anything. Sexually, he was as attuned to her body as he could ever be to another person's. The prudishness that had infected him during their early years together had entirely dissipated. She had taught him to be sexually uninhibited, and he had learnt to respond. But recently, their sex life had dipped. They were a little bored with each other. It was understandable. But she could still elicit desire in him. Despite all the familiarity of their physical life, she could still surprise him by her behaviour, just as she did now by some subtle opening up. Perhaps it was because he'd been out. His absence had evoked some sort of insecurity in her; she wanted to retain her rights of possession over him. Whatever the reason, he complied willingly enough. In the missionary position they thrashed about, more like mechanical toys than human beings, his legs between her bulky thighs, his head next to hers, looking away, panting on to the pillow, his mind oddly congested with wild, inconsequential thoughts. He finished and got off to wash.

When he climbed back into bed, she asked, 'Was it good? Was it good for you?'

This was unusual. She lived a contented if complacent life, secure in his fidelity. Before he could respond, the phone rang. He went downstairs.

'Hello.' Came a familiar voice. 'I rang to thank you for the evening.' How did she get his number? He was sure he hadn't given it to her. 'This time I'd like to invite you out,' she said.

They met in St James Square, and from there the woman took him to an expensive hotel where they made love. The sex was as sweet as the complimentary Belgian chocolate the hotel provided. Afterwards, they dressed and left, splitting up as soon as they had exited the plush lobby.

That night, when she turned off the light, his wife rolled over and demanded her conjugal rights. She did the same thing the night after,

Coconuts Kill More People Than Sharks

and the next night. At the height of their love-making, on the fourth evening, his wife started laughing, even as he continued, like Thumper the Rabbit. Why should he take his unwonted good fortune for granted? When they had finished, Wilson lay there thinking. His wife was as unaccountable as when he had first met her. He found himself getting out of bed even before the phone started ringing.

'It's past midnight,' his wife said. 'Who can it be?'

'Probably Henry,' he said, referring to his old friend, who had become a regular alibi.

'Is he all right? He's not in any trouble, is he?'

The phone continued ringing. He really didn't want to lie any more than he had done already, and so with the merest of hesitations, Wilson was able to say:

'I'll just get that, shall I?'

He managed to get to the phone just before it stopped ringing.

'Can't you ring me at work?' he asked.

'I just rang to ask you out,' said the woman.

'It doesn't make it any easier when you ring me at home,' he said. 'In fact, I'm wondering if we should carry on.'

He said this without thinking, emboldened by sexual satiety. Why should he risk it all for this phantom? After all, that was what she was, wasn't she? Well, they weren't in love, were they? Nor, in truth, was he with his wife.

'I want to meet you, that's all,' she said.

Well, he supposed he owed her that. What was more, the salubrious environment she took him to was not to be sniffed at. After all, you only lived once.

She asked him to meet her in Vauxhall.

'I want you to meet me near the cold store,' she told him. Wilson was there at the appointed hour. It was a concrete fastness, with grey skies overhead, and a whipping wind off the Thames. The traffic snarled and cruised around; there were not many people about. He saw her drive up to the apron outside the massive cold-storage building and stop her car. She waited in the driver's seat while he went over. He felt his steps took a long time. The window descended, and he saw that she had been crying.

'What's the matter?' he asked.

'I'm your dream,' she said. 'Don't you understand that?'

He stood there, feeling awkward in the chilly air, his trousers flapping around his thighs, feeling small, and ridiculous. What was she getting at? If she was a dream, she was an impossibility. What could be simpler than that? He had to choose clay, didn't he? He had to choose certainty, mediocrity, even. Wasn't that the safer course? What choice did he have?

She took her hand away from the black steering wheel and extended it out of the window. Her arm was long, thin, and naked. He took her palm. It was warm. He didn't like to make decisions. His wife had taken an interest in him, and he had been happy to go along with it. One thing led to another, and now here was, twenty years later, a middle-aged man no less fortunate than millions like him. The hand was withdrawn.

'Is this goodbye?' she asked.

'I don't know.'

Something had to happen. Either she would drive away, or she would stay. At any rate, one of them had to say something.

'Well, all I can say is I'm disappointed,' she said.

'You're married, too,' he said.

She glanced up at him with unmistakable contempt.

'You've missed a great opportunity,' she said.

'What? To destroy my marriage? Why did you call me at home?'

'You dreamed me!' she said angrily. 'I'm only here because of you.'

She sat naked, her knee-high white leather boots resting on the cheap fabric of the seat. She was real. It was a windy London afternoon.

'OK, I did dream you,' he conceded. 'But you're real enough. So's your car. So's the sex.'

'You wouldn't have dreamed me if I wasn't needed,' she said. 'Have you ever considered,' she said, knitting her brows, 'that the life you call real is just a dream? I point the way you should go.'

'How can I trust you?' he said. 'I don't know you. I don't even know your name.'

'My name is Lilith,' she said.

'Well, it's been nice knowing you, Lilith,' he said.

She nodded and accelerated away. He watched as her car stopped to make way for the heavy traffic, and then, with a flash of brake lights, it moved behind a bendy bus and disappeared.

He opened the front door of his house, calling out cheerily in his usual manner, 'I'm home!' There was no response. Upstairs he found one half of the wardrobe empty. The house was as neat and spruce as it had ever been. Only one thing was missing: his wife. There was no note, nothing. That night, he opened a tin of beans and ate it from the can, uncooked. He padded to the bathroom for a wash and went to bed. There was complete silence. He wondered if the phone would ring. But it didn't. He listened to the stillness. The other half of the bed was cold, so he curled into a foetal position on his side. It was strange to be sleeping there all alone. He closed his eyes. Images of the dream girl appeared to him but made no sense. In the morning he awoke and went to work, his mind numb. He returned, as before,

to an empty house. Just before nine, the phone rang. It was his wife. He had never felt so relieved in all his life.

'I just wanted to say,' she said, croakily, 'I've made a terrible mistake.'

'It's OK,' he told her. 'Just come home.'

When she returned, lugging two cases, they flung into each other's arms. He enjoyed the warmth of her body against his, and the emotional relief almost made him weep. Soon he was kissing her, uninhibitedly on the mouth, which he hadn't done for ages. They were both excited and made love immediately. Afterwards, he felt so happy he could hardly speak. They made love again and fell asleep, where they lay, like adolescents, in the living room, their clothes scattered about, the suitcases still unpacked. During the entire night he did not wake once, nor, as far as he knew, did he dream. He listened to his wife's untroubled breathing beside him, rolled over, and kissed her gently on the cheek. What right did he have to expect anything more out of life? Wasn't he, when all was said and done, a very fortunate man? He sighed contentedly. He lay, his eyes open for some time, staring up at the ceiling, and rolled over on to his side, just as the phone began to ring. His wife carried on breathing as before, dead to the world. He waited while the phone rang on and on until finally, it stopped. He went downstairs to watch TV and take a nip of brandy. He sipped the fiery liquid while watching *The Magnificent Seven*.

When the phone rang again he snatched it up and shouted, 'Just leave me alone, can't you?'

'It's me, old man. I just wanted to ring up and say sorry.'

'Who is this?'

'Don't you recognise my voice, old man? It's me. Henry. Do you want me to come round and explain?'

'That won't be necessary.'

'OK. Well… thanks. I hope we can remain friends, that's all.'

'Sure, why not?' he found himself saying.

When he put the phone down, he realised how clever his wife had been. She knew he was having an affair because she had been seeing Henry herself, probably during the daytime, while he was out at work. Did it matter? Perhaps now, if Henry was out of the picture, they might get on better. At around dawn with the birds starting to sing and the sky lightening to mauve, he went upstairs and tried to sleep. Something was not right. Somewhere in the software of his brain a worm was coiling, spreading unrest and unfulfillment. But he would live with it. He had to. Life was a matter of choices, after all.

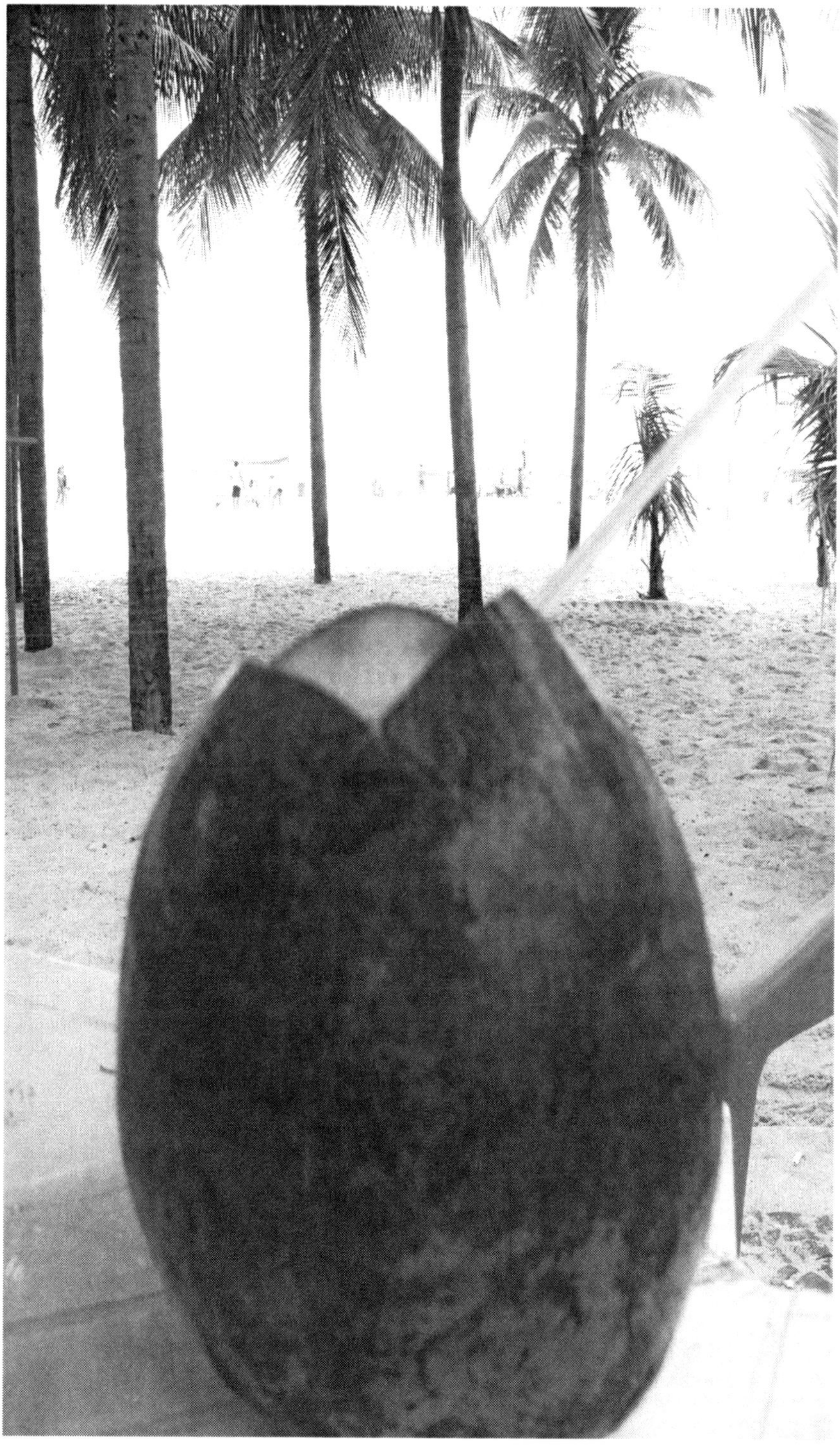

THE MAN WHO KEPT PANTHERS

Now I call myself a reasonable man. It was like this. I have a flat. A one bedroom flat. Small bathroom. Small kitchen. Bedroom. Lounge. A bit of damp coming through here and there – can't be helped. Nicely furnished. I never like anyone to live in any of my places where I could not live myself. I always deal with the tenants myself. Man to man. Or man to... woman. Not that there's any of that. No. Never. I even steam-clean the carpets! Between tenants! And I put in a washing machine. I look after the rates. And the water rates. What have you? There you are.

When it comes to choosing a tenant, I hardly ever go wrong. Except once. Yes, once.

Anyway, I do the interviewing myself. I never leave it to an agent. I meet everyone. I look at their faces. Into their eyes. I think I can tell people, know what I mean? I hardly ever make a mistake. That is, until he came here....

I should have known something was up. You see, they had been moving them into the block. The loonies. Spilling them from the mental hospitals. 'Care in the community,' they called it. Well, he didn't come from the council. But still, never mind. Anyway, there he was.... I'll never forget it.

Eric: Good morning!

Me: 'Morning! Mr Jones, isn't it?

Eric: That's right!

Me: I showed him, the previous tenant, everything. I looked into his eyes. Nothing wrong there.

Eric: Brown eyes.

Me: But he was gone. Up there. A loony. I should've known it. The flat, I told him, was small. Very small.

Eric: That's all right. I haven't got much stuff.

Me: Working, are you?

That's the first question I always ask. No point taking in the unemployed. It takes too long to get the housing benefit. Once I had an Irish couple living here. All twenty of them. Each signing on at the dole. A whole army of invisible people. All called Smith. I wasn't going to make the same mistake again. So here he was... Eric. He seemed perfectly OK. Now after I've got the deposit and rent in advance I never go near the place. Direct debit. Straight into the bank. No need, you see. But sometimes, if something needs doing, or if I'm passing, I might pop in... so I did, about six weeks after. He wouldn't let me in... and that's when I noticed it. A pong. A slight pong.

Me: You haven't got any animals in there, have you?

Eric: No.

Me: I did tell you, didn't I, no animals allowed? Because the flat is too small you see, and the neighbours.

Eric: No, I've got no pets.

Me: That's fine then... fine.

So I went away. He exited. But then I came back.

Me: What did you say you did?

Eric: What?

Me: I mean, for a living.

Eric: I'm an accountant.

Me: Ah good, that's good.

So I went away. But I came back. Something wasn't right. I went round there. One night. I looked through the living room window, just to check everything was all right. And that's when I saw it. A pair of eyes. Animal's eyes. And white teeth. Fangs. Incisors. And I smelt this smell. Like you do when you're in the country. Shitty smell. Of shit. Manure or whatever. And sweat. Animal sweat. I was standing there thinking about the smell and then I realised: he had something in my flat! He was keeping an animal inside my flat! I went and knocked on the door. What else could I do?

Eric: Yes? Oh it's you, Mr Jones.

Me: Yes it's me. Are you keeping an animal in that flat?

Eric: Yes.

Me: Now, don't deny it - you are you say?

Eric: Yes. It's only temporarily.

Me: What kind of animal?

Eric: She's a panther.

Me: A panther? Don't be ridiculous!

Eric: Look for yourself.

So I looked. Sure enough, curled up there on the sofa – taking up most of the sofa – was an enormous, black panther. Apparently asleep. Strangely enough, I couldn't smell the pong.

I said: 'I'll have to see about this.'

So I went away. I was going to ring the council or whatever. But instead I went back to the office. I was busy. I didn't make any calls. But that night as I was undressing I remembered. Then I fell asleep. And dreamt of panthers. In the morning I knew what I had to do. It was the best time. I went straight back there. It was my first call of the day. Eric was out. But some of the other tenants in the block were there. A loony was muttering to himself while walking home. I didn't want

David Del Monté

to let myself in with my key. But I had to. And sure enough, there she was. On the sofa. A large, black, panther breathing softly in and out, its hind legs hanging off the end, its enormous jaws moving slightly as it slept. I stepped out, closing the door softly behind me. I went upstairs and sat down at my desk. I took out a pen and paper. And began to write a Notice To Quit.

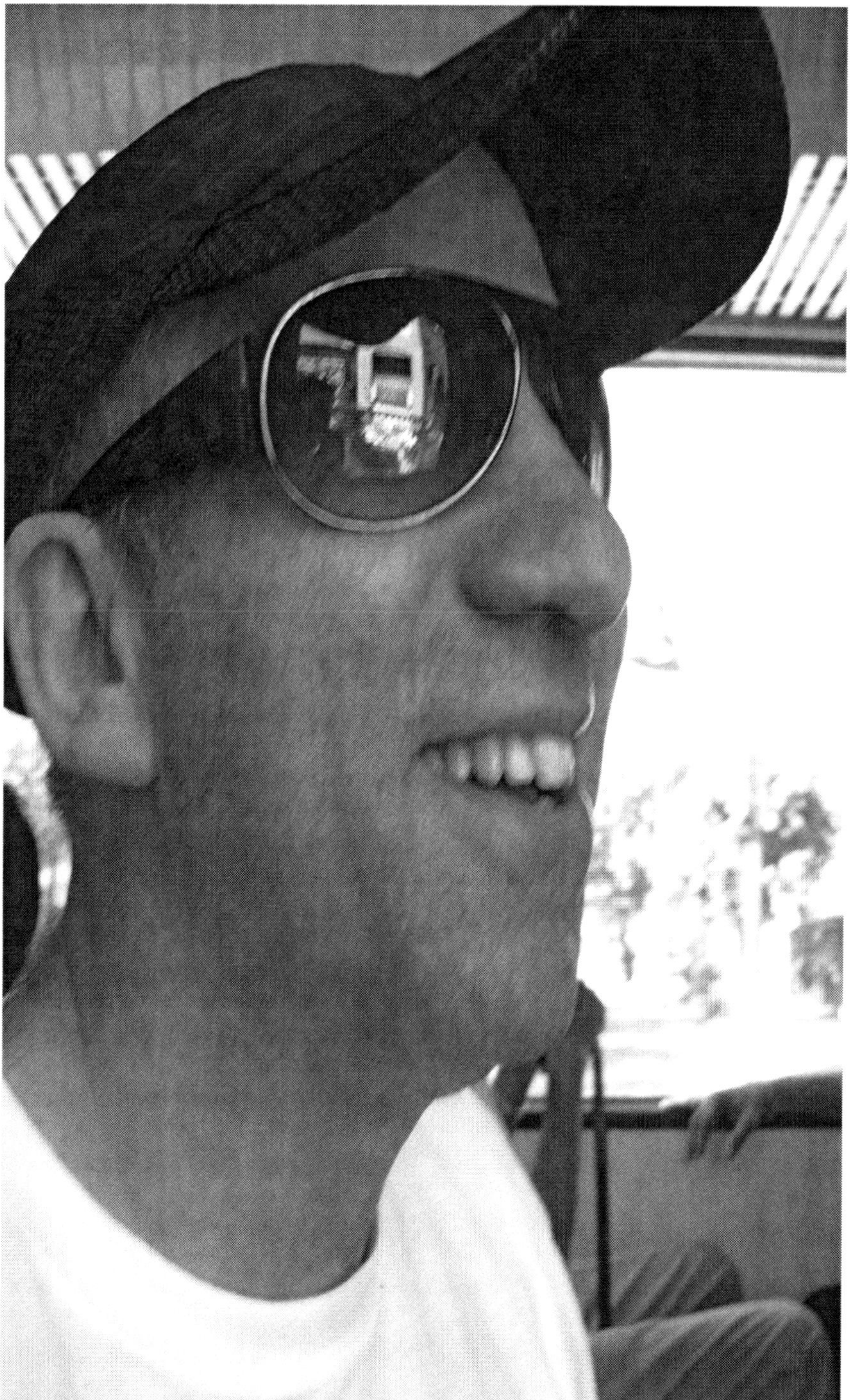

ANIMAL RIGHTS

It started innocuously enough in the 1970s and '80s.

The animal rights lobby at that stage was a vocal, radical, and splinter group, unable to inflict any real harm on the political establishment. They were a nuisance none-the-less, raiding animal laboratories, sabotaging hunts, and scaring fisherman away from riverbanks. That in essence, was the entirety of it.

All of this, I am aware, Jon, will appear deeply ironic to you, as you look back from the vantage point of the mid twenty-first century and view the cityscape from your eighteenth-floor editorial suite. You will remember me, of course. I am Gerard. Gerard Cross. Remember Gerard Cross, Jon? No, don't reach for that phone. I am far away, and this has been sent to you by messenger. I am fifty-five years old. I have spent most of my adulthood fighting for animal rights, as you know. But I am on trial, as I am sure you know, for violating the constitution, for betraying the revolution, the animal rights revolution, which came into being, I would say in January 2110, not March Jon, following the environmental upheavals caused by the spreading of the Ozone hole throughout the world.

I admit, Jon – and you can print this – that I was one of a dedicated clique intent on giving animals a better future. I was never, however, part of that radical wing which has led the peoples of the world to starvation. If the animal censor allows that to remain, let me lay out before you the parameters of the debate, as it took place in those heady days of the1990s, some twenty years before any of us had any idea that we would come to power.

The debate centred on the problem of knowing when to stop. Granted, that if a law was passed forcing everyone to become vegan, then the pastures given over to dairy herds and the like could be put at the disposal of pulse production. That can all be taken for granted, and none of us in the party had any problem with that. Of course, no one could have anticipated the president's discovery, when, in 2115, he exclaimed over breakfast, 'Pulses feel pain too!' and thenceforth forbade the eating of pulses.

The real problem, in my view, lay in the passing of the animal property laws. If animals were to be given full rights, it was argued, these should include the rights of abode. The turning over of the mass of our agricultural land in the 2020s had, as is well known, disastrous results. Minks and foxes ran wild, and what remained of domestic animals were killed.

When I faked my death in 2021, by hologram, I did so because I intended to go underground and sabotage the animal rights patrols which were empowered by law to enter every home, hunt down, and kill any person found to be eating animals or animal produce. Cases of pensioners being mown down by machine guns for eating boiled eggs became widespread. But the population cowed beneath a militant and ruthless political machine, which brooked no opposition.

Future generations, should they succeed in ridding themselves of this ideological and fanatic clique, may be hard put to understand how on earth such a grouping succeeded in seizing political power in the first place. The answer I give you is contained in one word: ruthlessness. The animal rights party, of which I was one-time secretary, was zealous, disciplined, and prepared to go to any lengths to bring about its objectives. Once in power, it simply liquidated any person or organisation opposed to it.

Of course, accession to power was helped by the coincidental events surrounding the mass suffocation of 1000 lambs on their way to France, and the destruction of 300 dairy cattle in a landslip in Wales. But what really brought the party to prominence was its success in winning the battle for the hearts and minds of the people – a battle begun in the 1970s and '80s when videos depicting the suffering of animals in slaughterhouses were shown for many years to every school-age child in the country.

The animal rights patrols, set up in the first place to safeguard the well-being of animals, rapidly became more militant. Children, briefed by decades of our propaganda, were quite prepared to inform on anybody harbouring the odd chicken, cow, or horse. Fishermen, of course, had long had their peace disturbed, and all the trawlers had long been broken up for scrap.

The one single trait which distinguished the animal rights activist from his human rights campaigner was our party's manifest dislike of the human race and our determination to see the human being brought down to where he belonged: at animal level, or as it has turned out, below animal level.

Thus the virtues of matriarchal societies and the early gatherer societies (the word 'hunter' having been excised from common folklore) became part of the national educational curriculum. I fell out with my colleagues over the animal property rights law. I faked my death by the simple expedient of having myself filmed falling from party headquarters and disappearing through a grille in the sewer below. It was then transmitted one afternoon when all the politburo was on the Commons tea-room balcony, along with sound effects. It had everyone fooled and gave me five years during which I wreaked hundreds of acts of sabotage on the party and, as my enemies would say, the country.

I would say, Jon, that by this time, the very existence of certain species was in doubt. People were forbidden to keep chicken, sheep, cows or any animal destined for slaughter. So the production of those animals lost its raison d'être. Those animals which survived and were kept in sanctuaries rapidly fell prey to those predators against whom culls had previously been practised.

By the end of the second five-year plan, no one dared to be found eating chicken, eggs, beef, veal, fish, milk, butter, cheese, or any animal derivative for fear of outright execution by the animal rights patrols. It has been estimated that Britain lost an eighth of its population this way. The remainder, afraid and cowering, gave up eating animal foods in any shape or form.

However, for me, the property laws were too much, and I went underground. The only person I let into my confidence was my girlfriend, and I can name her now because she is dead, killed under torture when animal investigators discovered my death. Even you, Jon, sincerely believed I had died, but your joking about it never offended me. I knew you had to keep in with 'them.' Unfortunately, the truth filtered out. It came after reports of my deeds filtered back to my erstwhile colleagues and they launched an investigation. The grille through which I had fallen was studied and it was soon ascertained that its aperture was too small for me to pass through and that the hologram image of myself had been necessarily reduced.

I was arrested eating steak along with several other overweight meat eaters, on a barge on the river Thames where a number of other outlaws were fishing.

I remember you, Jon, in the good old days. You always had a good shape about you. But now I urge you: eat! To be human is to inflict pain. And so I urge: eat! Eat all you can.

Yours sincerely,

G Cross

Ex-Counsellor, Animal Rights Party of UK

(ARPUK)

THE ANCHORITE OF GLASSFIBREVILLE

'Glass fibre has much to recommend it as a personal dwelling space,' so wrote Agnes Slocombe, Britain's first anchorite of Glassfibreville. 'Once in possession of glass fibre, and sufficient quantities of resin and hardener,' continues her account published in the *Hendon Times* on 13 April 1999, 'a personal space may be constructed that is very like a shell.' Shell, perhaps, is an apt description.

The origins of the anchorite who popularised this system of individual cell construction are not fully documented. What is known is that Slocombe realised the potential of the structure as a hermetic seal against the world. Legend has it that she preserved a rectangular piece of glass fibre, a small receptacle containing resin, and a tube of hardener; in order that when the time came and she found the pollutants in the air and the moral decay all around her overwhelming, she might be sealed forever within her home, which would then become her catacomb.

Like all great thinkers ahead of her time, she was ridiculed, and her construction, erected in the garden of her then semi-detached house in what was then a suburb of London known as East Finchley, became subject to numerous visits from the local planning department of what was termed in those days 'The Borough.' Nothing could prevent her, however, from entering the small structure and for the remainder of her days she communicated, and was fed via a small aperture in her shell, which she maintained as the only communication between herself and the outside world. In time, of course, as we all know, the virtues of the structure, and the advantages it afforded as protection against the chemicals in the air, and of course, the pressures wrought by the world's ever-increasing population, led thinkers to reassess her role in the management of the world's housing stock.

Glassfibreville, as we know it, only started to grow up around the original structure when it was pointed out that the bricks and mortar (not to say wasteful use of wood for floorboards, et cetera) of the terraces were not viable to replace in original form. When glass fibre, as a construction, got the go-ahead, it was not long before thousands, and then millions, of like-minded souls were able to avail themselves of government supplies of fibre and resin, together with instructions of how to erect their very own anchorages.

Glassfibreville today is breathtaking to behold, and glass fibre is the acme of modern building materials, being light, incredibly strong, and versatile. Fly over Glassfibreville and the witness is overwhelmed by the sheer variety of colours with which the modern-day anchorites have seen fit to spray-paint their shells. Most are single cell, but some are more elaborate. None, of course, are quite as tiny as the original anchorite's. Where she is buried – correction – sealed, is a matter of dispute today, as her glass-fibre anchorage is lost among the tens of thousands that occupy the suburb once called East Finchley. What is now known is that, mocked as she was, condemned for being a railing delinquent wife, today the anchorite of Glassfibreville can be viewed as one of the greatest forerunners in the history of housing development. Glassfibrevilles have been replicated all over the world, and millions also retain a small panel of webbed fibre with which, aided by a small dab of a brush, they will seal their own doom. When done, recycling may indeed continue. Sealed structures are air-tight, watertight, and almost entirely indestructible. They can, should public morals allow, be used as buoys on the oceans, channels, or fairways, and thereby serve as beacons for shipping; or perform a task as fenders on the sides of great cargo ships, and so enable citizens to perform a useful role, in death, if not in life.

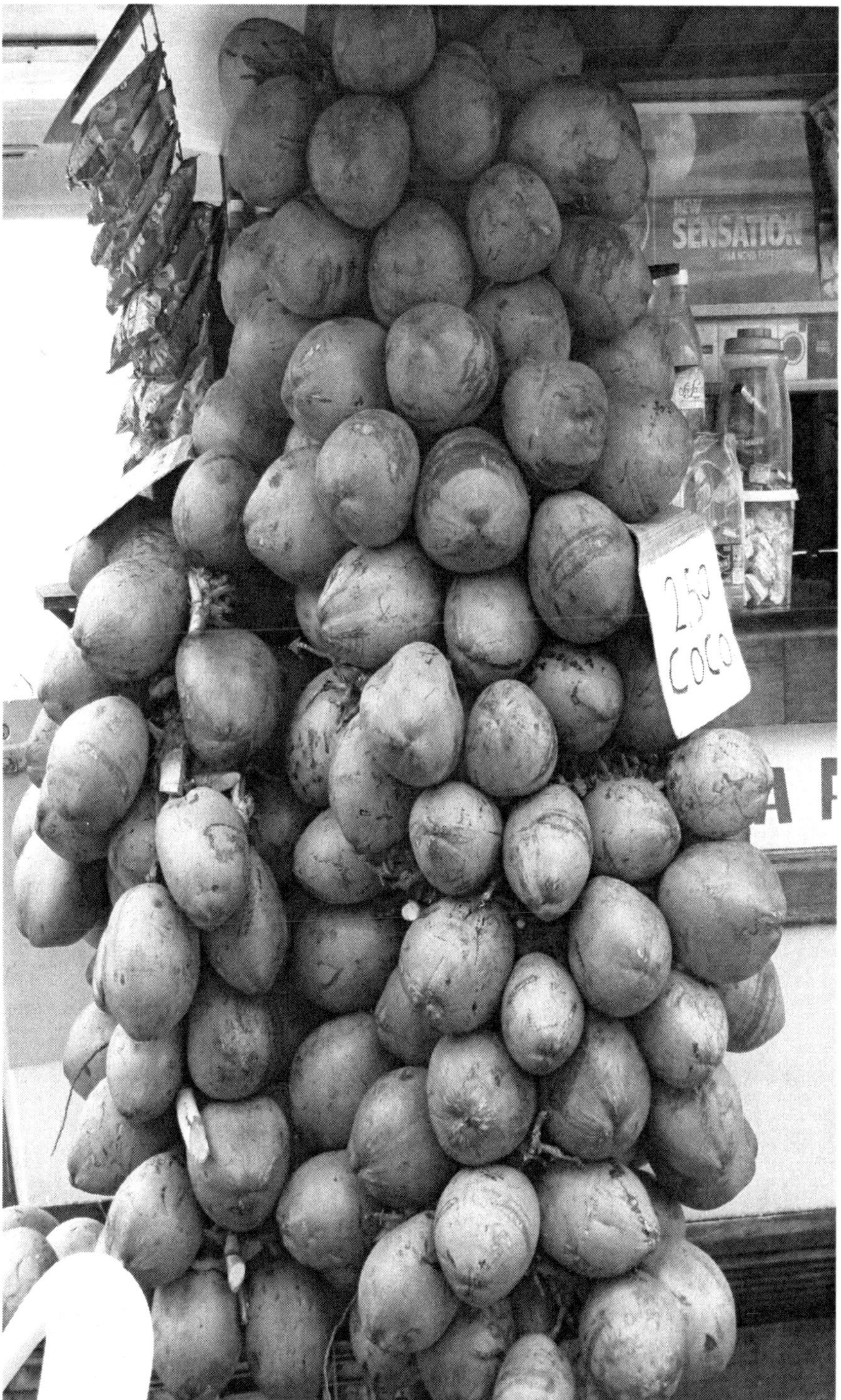
SENSATION
2,50
Coco

HONORARY CONSUL

In this province, where I am honorary consul, my compatriots die at an average rate of one a month. I have become so used to conducting the formalities, that the authorities have come to expect my presence beside the body as a matter of course. Although medically unqualified, I have been asked to provide death certificates. My compatriots being, in the locals' opinion, so disposed to drink, the services of a local doctor are considered irrelevant. At least, this is what I was led to believe. The authorities now look to me to take over the administrative burden completely, and I find that more of my time is being taken up in tracking down relatives, booking hotels , and bereavement counselling.

The local worthies purport to be completely baffled.

'Why do your people come here to die?' one asked. 'We have tourist attractions, ruins, beaches. But we have become a destination of death. Why?'

The speaker was an old friend of mine, an Indian man of indeterminate age; he could have been anything between sixty and eighty. He was small, slender, with a bald brown head and a sweet little face devoid of wrinkles, except around the eyes, where they fanned out like bats' wings. His lips were liver-coloured and his teeth a dark beige. If you put him against certain shades of wallpaper, the kind at the maharajah's palace, for example, he would be totally invisible.

'Why do people come here to die?' I echoed. 'It's quite simple, really. They're bowled over by the beauty of the place.'

For that comment I received a tiny fluttering tap on the arm.

'Boris,' he said, 'You are joking, always joking!'

Yes, I was being a tad ironic.

He padded off in his little canvas slippers to find a servant to bring us some *lassis*. It was two o'clock in the afternoon. The veranda on Mr Pugh's bungalow was very pleasant. A palm cast its fronds in our direction, affording us some much-needed shade. In any case the bungalow was so placed in its proximity to the sea, that it picked up all the available breeze, slight as it was.

I sat on the lounger and regarded the Strip where most of the 'Action' took place. It was indeed a sordid place. A congested square mile of cheap stalls and booths offering anything from souvenirs to *qat*, this small coastal area was a magnet for young people, especially from my country. Why did they come? I wished to God they wouldn't.

It made my life irksome. Of course if it had not been for my sense of humour, as Mr Pugh once put it, I would not be consul. But here I was, fetched up in Awlpindi because I was once stopped at the airport. The customs opened my suitcase and found thousands of scratch-cards. They came to the unlikely conclusion that I was a missionary. But I suppose I was, in a way. When the curious customs officers won a prize (surprise, surprise!), I was urged to spread the largesse to relatives and friends who appeared from nowhere like woodlice. My enforced generosity necessitated setting up a lottery to get some of my money back. That was ten years ago. Now the place is a hive of itching and scratching. I try to remember if Awlpindi has changed since my arrival. I would have to say that, on balance, it has. My main import was greed. Of course, greed is innate in every man. But in Awlpindi it was only latent. They worshipped their gods in a childishly anthropomorphic way, placing little heaps of rice on leaves and depositing these offerings everywhere. The people were serene, quite untouched by the need to acquire possessions or 'Get on in the world.' I wonder if the Strip would have developed but for the scratch cards and lottery that Boris Strowlovsky introduced. No, when I first arrived, there was no Strip, there were no Lebanese businessmen selling hashish and shoddy trinkets, and there was no alcohol, the by-product of the lottery prizes that the locals would not drink. When I think about it, I suppose I brought the recipe to Awlpindi; others have mixed the brew.

'So, my good friend,' said Mr Pugh, carrying a tray of *lassis*, unable, it seemed, to find his servant, 'you haven't answered my question.'

'Why my people come here to die?' I said. 'It is all you offer them,' I said.

Mr Pugh looked perplexed.

'Can you think of one foreigner who has settled here, married, been accepted?'

Mr Pugh pointed at me.

'Mr Pugh,' I said, 'I'm a bachelor. And you know why I am here.'

Mr Pugh shook his head and handed me a frothing *lassi*. I began to drink the sweet yellow liquid. It was most refreshing.

'Money,' I said.

'That is very sad, Mr Boris.'

'Not for me,' I said. 'This week I think I have got back to where I was when I first arrived. Soon I will be able to return to my country. But like everyone else, I don't want to return. I enjoy the pace of life here. And the heat.'

'Mr Boris,' said Mr Pugh. His lips looked more liverish than usual and his eyes even darker and sadder than before.

'I am sorry to inform you, but you do realise there will be a tax to pay.'

'A tax to pay?'

'Oh yes.'

I sighed and finished my *lassi*.

The breeze wafted against my cheek. The sea glittered in the distance. I could hear the faint hum of traffic on the Strip and see the tiny black ants of tourists wandering from booth to booth, in search of fulfilment, or worse. Awlpindi was a place you never left. Somehow I did not really care.

'You understand, of course?' Mr Pugh said, sitting close to me and solicitously resting his small brown hand on my large, thick arm.

'I understand, of course.'

'You are not minding?'

'No, I am not minding.'

'I think,' said Mr Pugh standing up and adopting a brighter tone, 'I know why they die!'

'Oh yes?' I said looking up.

'They are like you, Mr Boris. No family!'

That pleasant balmy evening I strolled down from Mr Pugh's bungalow to the Strip. I milled with the crowds of youngsters from Astrakhan, Moscow, Petersburg, Odessa, and beyond, with their cut-off shorts and cheap sandals as they browsed from stall to stall. I suppose, given the numbers, the mortality rate was no worse than back home. I stopped at one booth which, oddly, was displaying no products.

'*Da?*' asked a small boy sitting in a white short-sleeved shirt.

'What are you selling?' I asked.

He produced one of my scratch cards – or a very good copy of it.

I looked at it. I was rather annoyed. This was not an authorised retailer. I asked how much. The price he gave me was exorbitant – four or five times the going rate. I paid up, however, in order to gain the evidence, and was going to put the card in my pocket when the boy motioned to me to hand it back. When I did so he scratched it furiously.

He smiled.

'You so lucky!' he said, 'You win first prize!'

'You don't say?' I said.

'Really!' he said, excitedly.

He was a good actor, I thought. He disappeared beneath his counter, re-emerging seconds later. I was expecting the usual bottle of vodka or a cheap trinket. What I was given was a small matchbox. This he handed to me, with a smile. I opened the matchbox and saw a small pile of white powder.

I climbed back up the hill to Mr Pugh's. I found him on the veranda. I dropped the matchbox into his lap.

'Is this your idea of tax?' I asked.

'If the foreigners like it, why not?' he said.

'I can't say I have seen much evidence of public spending,' I said. 'I don't see any new schools or hospitals built with the money from the tourists,' I said. 'The place is disgusting. Litter everywhere. Rats.'

'Are you angry because someone broke your monopoly?' said Mr Pugh, in his irritatingly serene way.

'I think I will leave Awlpindi,' I said. 'I don't want to be honorary consul any longer.'

'As you wish,' he said.

For the first time since I had known him, Mr Pugh did not rise from his chair to see me off.

I walked down the hill. When I got to the Strip, it was dark and the place looked worse under the dim electric lamps than it had during the day. The place was still crowded with giggling young people. A few had lit fires on the beach. No doubt some would be sniffing the contents of matchboxes, or worse. First prize indeed! Perhaps when I returned to my apartment, there'd be a message on my answerphone, asking me to go to this or that hostel, to view this or that body, to write the death certificate, to contact the relatives, to organise the burial and the sending home of effects, a rucksack perhaps, a watch, or a few hundred dollars in travellers cheques.

I walked on to the beach and stood at the perimeter of a group of youngsters. There was a smell of hash and of meat burning. There was laughing, but as the night wore on things calmed down. The fire became embers, and the revellers lay down to sleep, or sat in a stupor, their heads slumped between their shoulders. I wondered if they felt as

I did, stuck between two cultures, unable to stay, unable to return. In those circumstances a short sybaritic life was perhaps to be preferred.

I walked along the shore and listened to the waves' rhythmic sounds. Usually such an accompaniment fed my soul and made me happy. Tonight it just made me sad. I returned to my flat, found the answerphone contained no messages, and slept until dawn. In the morning I packed my effects – not very many even after ten years – and took a taxi to the airport. There I joined some travellers returning after their holiday.

'Had a good time?' I asked.

'It was great,' a teenager replied.

'What did you like best?' I asked.

'The swimming,' she replied. 'What about you?'

'I was just passing through,' I said.

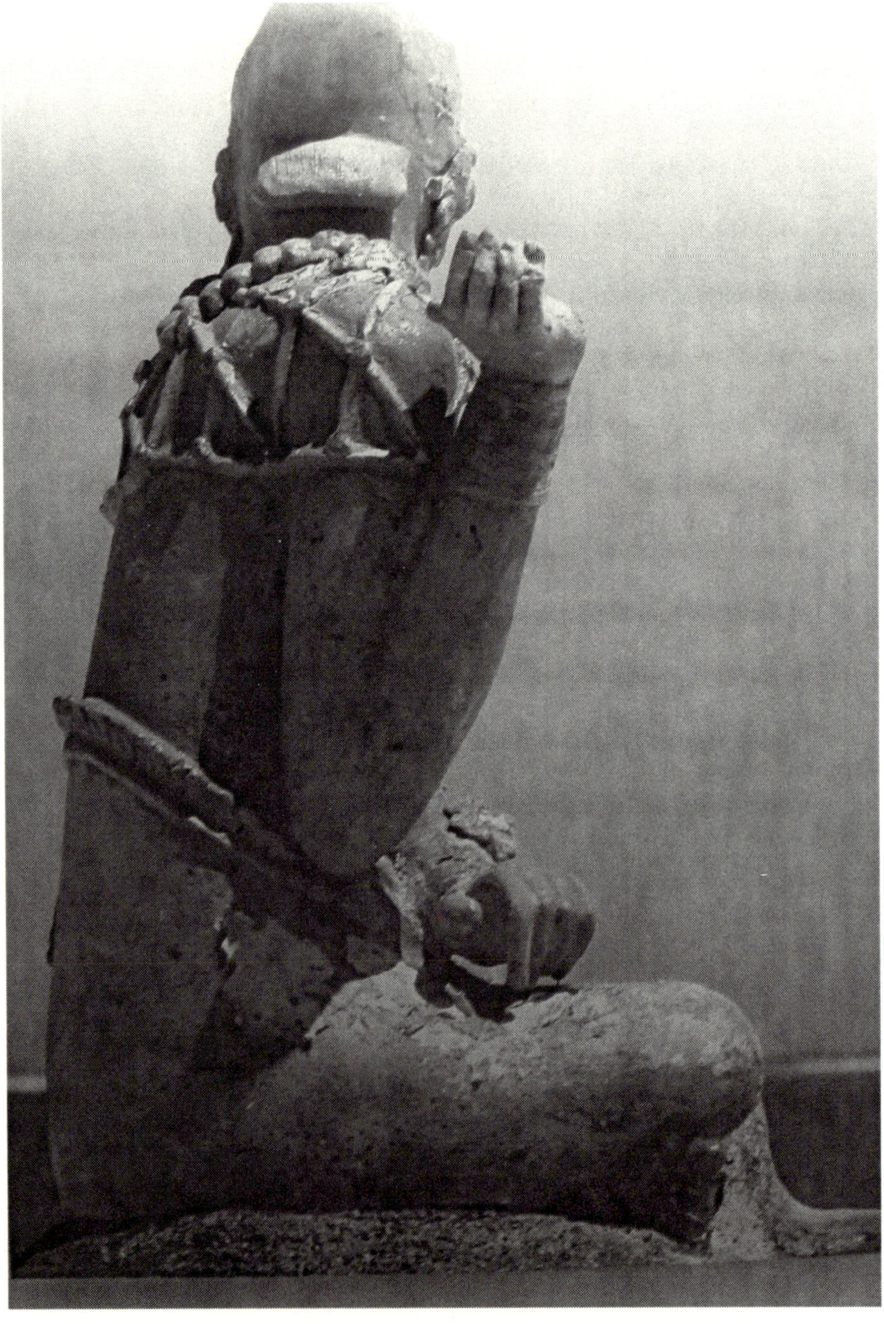

HOUSE

The day before Fred Hilton bought my house I was furious. That reaction wasn't right, I know. It was totally illogical. Yet as that house stood next to my parents', I knew it should have been mine.

I told my father: 'Dad, we should buy that house. It was last on the market two hundred years ago.' He laughed.

'Oh yeah?' he said. 'It hasn't got a bathroom. It hasn't got a kitchen. It's been used as offices.'

'Dad,' I said, 'I know that. I've passed that house every day of my life. I know it's been used as offices.'

'What do you want that house for anyway? You've got our house. Our house is your house. Use it as your own. Come and go as you please.'

'Dad,' I said (I was very young), 'it's not the same.'

'Not the same as moving out? You want to move out? Is that it? You want me to tell your mother you're moving out?'

'No, Dad, I'm not moving out. But if I bought that house, I would be next to you. We could put a hole in the wall and make connecting gardens; I could still come over every day. It would be like I was still there.'

'If you bought that house? If you bought that house? Am I hearing right here? With what are you going to buy that house? You haven't got a bucket to piss in. As God's my witness, have you done a day's honest work in your life? Can you put your hand on your heart, put your fingers into your inside breast pocket, take out your wallet, and hand me the deposit for that house? No, you can't fish out more than ten pounds. How the hell are you going to put down a deposit for that house?'

'I wasn't going to, Dad. I thought you might.'

'I might? I might?' He shook his head. 'You're very much mistaken, son, if you think that I would buy that house. What good would it do? You lie around all day. You're a bum, aren't you? A bum.'

'If you say so.'

'If I thought it was a good buy, I would buy that house.'

'Dad, it is a good buy,' I said. 'We can make an extension and build a kitchen and bathroom, and then I'd move in...."

He cut me off. 'It's out of the question.'

So Fred Hilton bought my house, at a snip, I might add. And what did he do? 'He proceeded to build an extension and put in a kitchen and bathroom, just as anyone would do. Over the last twenty years, Fred Hilton has married and raised two children in that house. As for me, I've been very happy, on the whole. I stayed with my parents. Dad was right, of course. His house was perfectly big enough. I could come and go as I pleased. As Fred Hilton's children started growing up they would scale the wall on our side and on one occasion little Sammy dislodged some tiles from our roof at the gable end, which sloped down very low, almost to the lawn. I have to admit I screamed at Sammy. Perhaps I overreacted when I grabbed him by the arm, swung him off the wall, and dropped him over on the other side.

'Never!' I said. 'Never climb on that wall again, do you hear?'

He went running back to Fred, and seconds later Fred appeared on a stepladder at the border wall, all ginger moustache and sandy hair.

'What's all this about Sammy?' he asked.

So I told him what had happened and Fred said, 'You used unnecessary force. You almost wrenched his arm from its socket.'

'You should control him better,' I said.

That was the start of our feud with Fred Hilton. It was a very civilised fight, very British. No one said or did anything. I would sit in our garden listening to the raucous cries of Sammy and Lillian as they played in Fred's garden. I would watch as Fred worked on his house, painting the windows. I have to admit he did a great job with the extension. He really had a nice house, did Fred.

When I met Susan, my father said, 'You should have bought that house, you know.'

'Which house, Dad?' I said.

'The one next door. Look at the price of property now. The trouble with my son is,' he said, looking at Susan, 'he started late. He's got a good job but not enough for a proper pension. As for a mortgage if he buys anything now, he'll be eighty by the time he pays it off, that is if he can find an affordable house. That house next door is big. Where can you find a house like that on the market now? You can, but at a price. Now the best you can aspire to is a tiny flat. Tiny. Tiny rooms.'

But Susan just smiled and said, 'We'll manage.'

Dad winked at me and later said, 'Marry her. You're on to a good thing there. Her father will give you the money for a mortgage.'

'No Dad,' I said. 'We're going away.'

'Going away?'

'To Spain, Dad. We're going to open a bar in Grenada.'

'What about your mother?'

'I'll go and tell her.'

So that afternoon Susan and I climbed up the hill behind the cathedral to the cemetery. I placed three daffodils picked from our garden on mother's grave. Then we went to Dad's house, and I packed and we left that very evening.

I sent some postcards to Dad over the years. Finally I heard that Dad had gone into a nursing home. He had to sell his house and use the funds to pay for his care. I thought about buying the house when it came on the market, but it was just too expensive. When I went home to bury Dad, I passed our house and knocked on the door just out of curiosity. Who should come to the door but Fred Hilton's son, Sammy, very slender and tall with dark hair.

'Ah, I see,' I said. 'Mr Hilton has bought this house.'

The boy turned his head to the side.

'Dad,' he shouted.

Fred Hilton came to the door. He was much older. What was left of his hair had gone grey, his moustache still retained traces of sandy colour at the tips.

'Yes?' he said.

'Congratulations,' I said.

'What are you talking about?'

'This house. Well done. You'll be buying up the whole street next.'

'I haven't bought this house,' he snapped.

'He won't buy it,' said Sammy. 'he says it needs too much work.'

'I'm a surveyor. Did you know that? I'm here to conduct works for the new owner.'

'Who is the new owner?'

'The city corporation. They say it is a museum piece. They want to keep everything as it is. How long did your family own this house?'

'Two hundred years.'

'Pity you sold up. They're going to have a nice income from tourists.'

'It's OK. I live in Spain. I enjoy the weather.'

'As you like,' he said. 'I hope you'll excuse me. I must get on.'

He closed the door. I went to the city council Recreation and Amenities Department to obtain details, and the man behind the counter put on glasses, scoured some official ledger, took off the glasses, smoothed his shirt, looked up at me, and said,

'There's no museum planned for there. The proposal was voted down at last night's council meeting in favour of a drop-in centre for the young unemployed and drug abusers. Local residents are rather upset about it. From what I hear there was nothing in there but a load of 1920s crap, in any case. Is there anything else I can do for you?'

I shook my head and turned to leave. On second thought I dug in my pocket and faced him again.

'There is only one more thing,' I said. 'Perhaps you might have a use for these.'

I handed him my keys.

'What are these for?' he asked, holding the keys away from his body as if they were infected.

'Those are the front-door keys to your new drop-in centre,' I said. 'I may drop in myself from time to time.'

He seemed unsure how to react.

'You'd be welcome, I'm sure,' he said. 'But I don't think I can accept these. You would have to sign something. It would be better if you just hung on to them.'

'Or threw them in the river?'

He half-smiled at me, not sure if I was joking.

'Why don't you keep them, sir, as a souvenir to bring back memories?"

I looked at him and said I would. And I have.

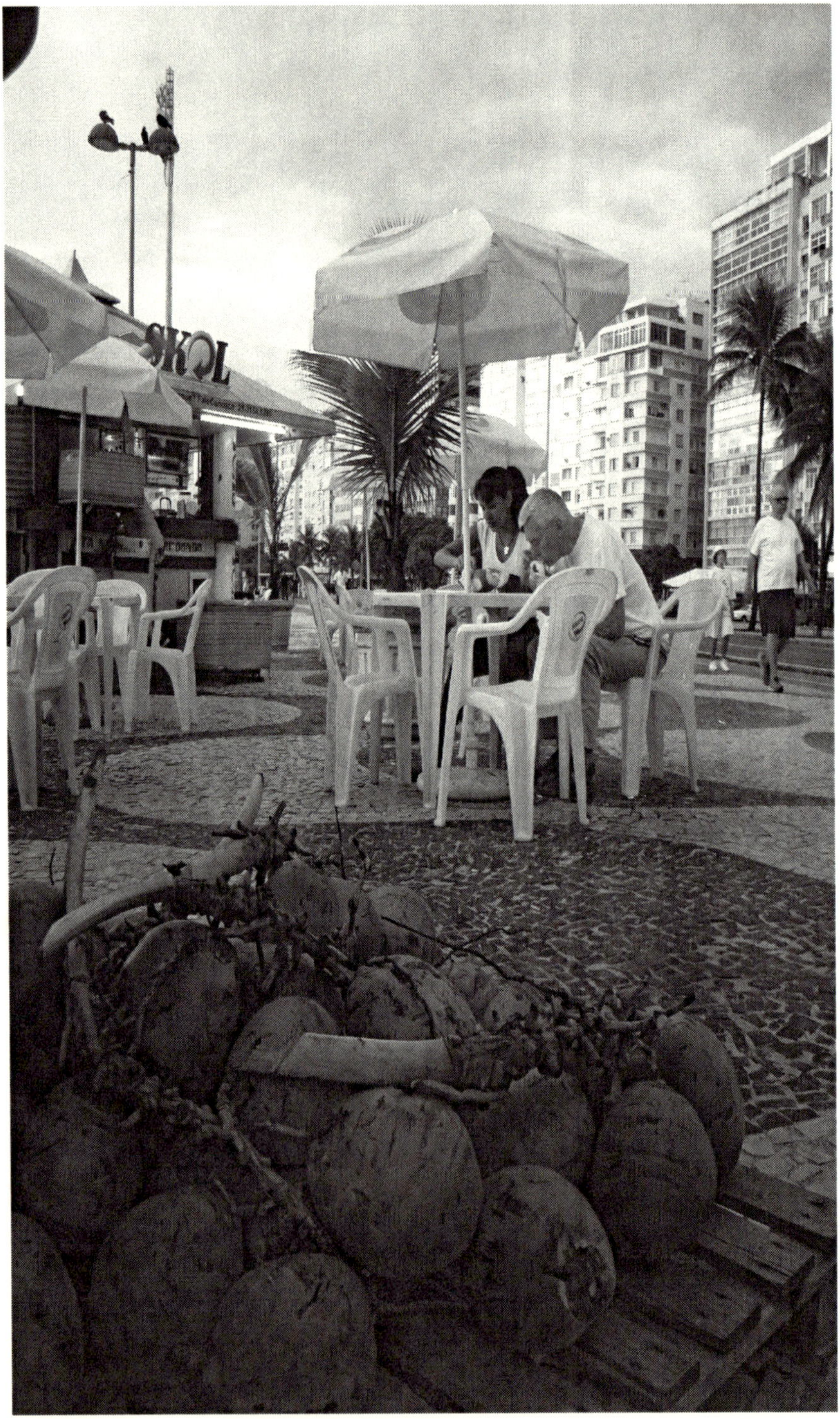
SKOL

MRS PHARAOH

Behind his back, we used to call him Pharaoh. To his face it was Mr Mohammed, and then suddenly, Ahmed. The first time I called him that it just slipped out unawares. I was carried away by the sight of his new purchase, a mansion attached to 1500 acres of pasture and gardens that rolled away into the wooded distance.

'It's just fantastic, Ahmed,' I said. Even though I was speaking to him via my mobile phone (he was in France on his helicopter and I was scared that I'd overstepped the mark). 'You don't mind if I call you Ahmed, do you?'

'If I can call you Prick,' he said.

Two weeks before, I had saved his four-year-old son from drowning in the Porchester municipal swimming pool. When Ahmed heard of my heroism, he paid me triple my lifeguard's salary to live on the estate and teach English to his son, eight-year-old daughter, wife, and servants.

The house was magnificent, draughty and period; as elegant a piece of Georgian architecture as could be found in those parts. Ahmed immediately determined to replace it with Ramses II vulgarity, complete with a mausoleum and a Louis XVI fountain on the front courtyard. For most of the day I was free to wander the grounds, take the horses for a canter, or just doss about. Ahmed was either in Paris, New York, or even London. But he never passed by the country. He would visit, when he had time, he said.

Architects and surveyors came by with their theodolites, took measurements; but nothing seemed to be happening very fast. The four-year-old was taken back to town as was the daughter, leaving only myself and Craddock, the housekeeper, on site. It felt as if we had been forgotten, but since our salaries were still being paid monthly into our accounts it seemed silly to leave. My natural indolence prevented me from moonlighting. During that summer I simply lay in the deckchair and watched the day labourers cut the grass in the paddock and take it away for hay. I did shopping on the net, using a Waitrose card that Ahmed's London office had sent me. Craddock and I wanted for nothing but good company.

In early August, I was awakened from one of my post-prandial slumbers by the arrival of a long sleek vehicle. I pushed back the straw hat, which had slipped over my nose. Emerging from the car was a female beanpole clad in a white trouser suit. Two eyes black and tiny as raisins peeped out beneath a floppy wide-brimmed hat. She closed the door awkwardly.

'You must be Johnson,' she said, when she reached me. 'No, don't get up.'

She looked over my head at the front door and then went on her way, her high heels click-clacking on the pebbles of the path. I jack-knifed out of the deckchair and was just in time to open the front door for her. She stopped, lowered her head so I could make out a long pale face, placed a white-gloved hand briefly upon my wrist, and passed by.

I went in after her.

'Can I help you?' I asked.

She was standing in the hallway looking up at the oak stairway that had already been earmarked for removal (and replacement by two high-speed lifts).

Without looking at me she said, 'Can you get my case from the car?'

There was a family of four Louis Vuitton leather-clad receptacles in the boot. I took them out and left them on the upstairs landing before joining Craddock in the kitchen. Mrs was in full flow.

'Good. I wish to be awakened at eight o'clock with a cup of tea, toast, and two eggs, boiled medium hard. Oh, and an orange juice.'

'Who does she think she is?' I remarked to Craddock when she had left.

'That's Mrs Pharaoh. It's money what makes her like that. But she's not a bad sort. Get on the net and order some provisions. Then go into the village for her highness' breakfast. I'll make up her bed. Go on then, look lively!'

In the morning, Mrs Pharaoh found fault with everything. The shower was too cold and too noisy, the horses had not been well looked after, and the house (she said) was dusty. That was hardly surprising, since we had no real help. But I just let her vent. Then Craddock made up a light lunch of celery and rocket salad taken from the walled garden. After that her highness announced that I was to take her riding. There were two horses in the stable, one of them a Shetland, the other a stallion. Mrs Pharaoh had me make up the stallion and accompany her on the Shetland. There was no contest. While she showed me a clean set of hooves I was left trotting aimlessly behind. Mrs circuited the paddock three times before I had gone halfway round. She laughed when she saw me, my legs almost reaching to the ground. She herself was got up in proper riding gear, jet black jacket, hat, hair braided back.

'You do look ridiculous!' she said before galloping off. Back in the tack room she told me she intended to take me into town that very afternoon and buy me some more 'appropriate' clothes, provided I act as her chauffeur. In the event, she sat in the front seat while I drove.

'Where to?' I asked when we got to the main road.

'Bunton,' she said.

'We won't find riding clothes in Bunton.'

I could see her bridling slightly at being gainsaid.

'High Fleeting might be better,' I proffered.

'How far?'

'Twenty miles, as the crow flies,' I replied.

'And as you drive?'

I shrugged and accelerated away. The car was responsive as silk. We drove in silence, she looking at her nails, while I negotiated the bends. We arrived at High Fleeting at around 4.00 p.m. and Mrs asked if we might first stop for a tea. It was pleasant to walk down the high street together. No one knew us. We might have passed for man and wife, except for the mismatch in our attire. There was an age difference between us. I was thirty; she was perhaps early forties, but no one would have guessed it. We found some old-fashioned tea rooms and waved away any queries from the elderly spinsters who ran it by drinking our teas impatiently. During the tea, Mrs answered her mobile phone and spoke to several people in a foreign tongue, laughing frequently and showing her teeth. It made me uneasy to sit there opposite her, the infusion gathering on my saucer where I had spilt it, trying not to wonder whether when she laughed, she was really happy or putting it on just for show.

'Is that Arabic you're speaking?' asked one of the old dears. 'I hope you don't mind my asking, but my husband was in Palestine before the War, and so I...'

'I was speaking Farsi – Persian,' said Mrs.

'Oh, were you? How interesting!'

Mrs clammed up.

'We really must be going. We have quite a hectic schedule.'

'Oh I'm sure,' said the old bat. 'You Londoners always have.'

Mrs straightened her back and walked out on to the high street, with me following three paces behind.

The clothes buying stretched out until closing time. When she was done, I had ten outfits including casual, riding, formal dining, everyday, and several suits. I reckoned that the small men's outfitters had never seen such largesse. The credit card bill stretched into four figures. Mrs made me try everything on at least thee times and left behind two of the suits for alterations. Finally she paid and we walked out with me loaded with carrier bags. On the way back Mrs received a few more calls on her mobile.

When we reached the house, I said, 'I can't remember when I last went shopping.'

'You look as if you've been sleeping in those jeans for at least a year.'

It wasn't far from the truth.

Neither of us made any attempt to get out of the car until finally she said. 'Well, I am rather tired.'

As she was opening the door I asked her if she might like to go riding the next day.

'I must go back to London. My husband is coming, and I must meet him at the heliport.'

She closed the door and walked towards the house. I doused the headlights and collected my bags from the boot. I caught up with her at the front door.

'Would you like me to drive you?' I asked.

In the dark I could not make out her reaction.

'Of course, if you don't want to…' I prompted.

'It will be an early start,' she said in a prim no-nonsense tone.

'How early?'

'Leave at six.'

'Fine by me.'

'Good.'

Mrs vanished inside.

During the long journey into town, Mrs did not say a word. She lay back in the passenger seat wearing a black headscarf and even though it was still dark outside, a pair of black-framed sun glasses. With her pale face and bright lipstick she looked like a film star in mourning. Her black dress reinforced the impression. When we stopped at a service station for petrol, I tried to interest her in a coffee, but to no avail. We arrived at Battersea heliport just in time to see Pharaoh land.

Mr, as stocky as a pocket tank, was at least a foot shorter than Mrs. Grinning, he marched towards us carrying an attaché case, the whipping Thames wind blowing a few wisps of black hair across his face. I immediately noticed something was different about him. Until now two hammocks of flesh swung beneath Mr's chin. He must have had plastic surgery. Close up I could see the bags under his eyes were gone too. Mrs got out of the car in her usual cool languid way, and Mr reached up on his toes and kissed his wife on the cheek.

'Ten Chester Street, SW1,' he informed me through the open car window, before shuffling into the back seat with her.

He chatted in Farsi, and she smiled and nodded, enjoying his company just as much, I supposed, as she had enjoyed mine. Well, he was her husband, why should she not enjoy him? I saw his hand rustle the hem of her dress and pat a smooth naked knee.

When we reached Belgravia, they got out and closed the door, forgetting about me completely.

'Where to?' I asked, lowering the car window.

'Uh?'

My words reached Ahmed's ears, causing him to turn momentarily, before he reached the front door of his townhouse. Mrs stopped too, and put on her sunglasses.

'Do you need him, love?' Ahmed asked his wife.

'I don't think so,' she said non-committal.

'Have you his mobile in case you do?' he asked.

She nodded, but she remained looking at me, or at least, I thought she was.

'Suit yourself, but keep your mobile on in case either of us should need you,' Ahmed instructed.

They both retreated inside their house and closed the door. I drove down Park Lane and parked in Curzon Street. From there I went on foot to Shepherds Market and popped into a coffee shop. I was on my second latte when my mobile rang.

'Yeah?'

'It's me.'

The voice was low and soft, quite unlike the hard tone Mrs had employed to date.

'Can you come back and get me?'

'Sure.'

Mrs was waiting outside the front door when I arrived. She got in the car and sat back in the rear seat.

'Where to?' I asked.

'Anywhere.'

I drove down to the Embankment. Along the side of the Thames a couple of ships were moored. At my suggestion, Mrs agreed to stop for some refreshment. We had a choice between the Latino sounds of the 'Admiral' and the Eastern menu of the 'Medusa.' Once ensconced at a table, looking out over the brown waters, I waited for Mrs to unburden herself.

'Do you have a girlfriend, Mr Johnson?'

'No.'

'Any hobbies or interests?'

Nothing that would interest you, I thought.

'Where do you go when you want to enjoy yourself?'

'When I lived in London I used to go the pub with my friends. Ice-skating. Anything, really.'

'I've never done normal things like that. With Ahmed I live a very sheltered existence. I can have whatever I like, you know. I'm very lucky – as he keeps reminding me.'

'You're lucky to have such a lovely family,' I said. 'Your son is so cute.'

'I never see him, really. Nanny brings him up Then he'll be sent to prep school. Boarding. Where did you go to school, Mr Johnson?'

'Hackney.'

When the waitress came over, we ordered some oriental set lunches, hers the vegetarian set with rice and baby corn served in a little Japanese-style lunch box. I had the beef teriyaki. We washed it all down with beer.

While she was in the loo, her mobile, left on the table, sprang to life. First it vibrated its way to the edge of the table and when I picked it up to stop it falling off, it throbbed in my hand. My thumb must have pressed the answer button, for between my fingers came the voice of Pharaoh, like a voice from the grave.

'Raina?' it asked plaintively. 'Raina? Speak to me, Raina. I've been a fool. I'm sorry. Please come back. Let's start again. We can be a happy family. It's not over. I won't let that woman damage us any more, I promise. The passion is over. It's petering out, just like you said it would. You mean everything to me, Raina. I can't bear to see you upset. Raina? Raina?'

I put the mobile to my ear.

'It's me,' I said.

'Prick?'

'My name is Seth Johnson.'

'And that's what a prick is: a Johnson. Where's my wife? Oh never mind where.' Asserting his tone of command, he added, 'Put her on, can you?'

I didn't need to reply because Mrs was striding purposefully towards me. I held out the mobile but she refused it, palm out.

'Tell him he can speak to me when he's got rid of that slut he's fucking.'

'You're to stop…'

'I heard,' said Ahmed brusquely.

Mrs took the mobile from me and pressed the off button. Then she resumed her seat opposite mine, gave her hair a swish with a quick flick of her head, and downed the remains of her beer.

She was silent all the way back to the country. When we arrived, she rushed straight inside and upstairs to her room. When I climbed up the stairs after her, I could hear her weeping. Gently, I opened the door and walked in. She was lying on the bed, face down, very quiet and very still. I sat down next to her and placed a hand upon her shoulder. I stroked her black hair until I felt her body relax and saw her eyes close. When she seemed to be asleep, I bent down, took off my boots, and hoisted my legs on to the bed, shuffling up so that I was lying next to her. Her eyes immediately sprang open, almost as suddenly as Glenn Close's in the bath scene of *Fatal Attraction*.

'What do you think you're doing?'

'Resting. Do you mind?'

She stared at me for a few seconds.

'Get the fuck off my bed.'

'Sure.' But I did not move.

Her eyelids closed over the hard black coals. I was beat and let myself drift away. I woke to see Mrs arguing furiously in Farsi on the bedroom's land-line. She had changed into a nightie and dressing gown. Her hair was done up inside a yellow towel. It was still only 5.00 p.m.

Holding the phone in one hand, she turned to me and said, 'You stink. Go and take a shower.'

This last excited the caller immeasurably. I could hear tinny protests all the way from Mrs' en suite facility. I hoped the voice wasn't Ahmed's and then I realised it must be. And he thought… I grinned. Well, serve him right, the dirty bugger. Give him a taste of his own medicine, only that of course he didn't know that Mrs and I hadn't… well, we hadn't, not so much as touched, let alone kissed. After I showered I came back into the bedroom and sat on the bed next to her. She was off the phone now, and I hoped, more relaxed. From where she was sitting, her thigh was only an arm's length away. Then suddenly she put her arm around me, pushed me down on the bed, and fucked me.

I did as I was told. I had no idea what she liked, so I just let her get on with it. I felt pretty numb. It was the surprise, mostly. When she climaxed, which she did remarkably quickly, she just climbed off me and disappeared into the bathroom. Emerging, she hardly looked at me, and after a few moments I sloped off, without even saying good-bye. The après-screw was decidedly below par. Back in my own seedy room, I began to wonder if the episode had ever taken place.

To make things up and to show some real romantic effort, I had Craddock lay a table in the dining room, with candles and serviettes. The latter tut-tutted as she went about her job. Then she started on the meal, rustling together a meal of Lancashire hotpot with pea and ham soup to start with, like a real pro. When it was ready, I went upstairs to fetch Mrs. I found her in bed, smoking a cigarette and dressed in a pink towel dressing gown.

'Dinner's ready, ma'am.'

'Is it?' she tapped the ash onto the carpet.

'What's the matter?'

'You know very well what's the matter.'

I caught the warning tone in her voice. It was the voice of a woman who knew she had the right to speak in such a tone. It was at once proprietorial and peremptory. No riposte was required. The best tactic would be to jolly her along.

'Look, why don't you get up and get dressed in your best gown? Just for the show. Pretend you're a film star.'

The edges of her mouth flickered into a smile.

'You're sweet,' she said, holding out the cigarette for me to put out, somewhere.

I let her patronise me. After all she was my boss. Our coitus had been so brief and unexpected my emotions had hardly been touched. All I knew was that a physical sensation between my legs signified a long overdue use for my private part. I hoped my suggestion would do the trick. Unfortunately I was wrong.

'How can we go on like this? You know you're in danger now, don't you? He could have you killed. Are you afraid?'

She took a draw on her cigarette. She was highly tensed and fraught and probably wracked with guilt. I had been used as a revenge fuck, but hey, who was complaining, after all? Still, there are few things worse than an unhinged woman, especially after you've done your best to please her.

'I am sure it is not as bad as all that,' I said with typical British sang-froid. I said it with some aplomb despite the fact that at the back of my mind I was pondering some means of a making a quick escape if I had to.

'Well,' she said, stubbing out the cigarette, 'if we're going to be killed, we might as well be hung for a sheep as for a lamb.' By which, I expect, she meant that I was the lamb cutlet.

And with that she opened her legs slightly revealing a newly shaven jet black bush – a piece of heaven that I, as sure as hell, was not going to neglect. The way she sidled down in the bed immediately communicated itself to my prick, but before anything could happen, the hoarse voice of Mrs Craddock came wafting up the stairs like a bat's breath on a summer's day.

'Dinner's ready!'

'Oh well,' she said, closing her legs as quickly as a pair of scissors.

'Let's go for it.'

At the stroke of eight, Mrs came down the stairs like Norma Desmond in *'Sunset Boulevard'*, wearing a long evening dress.

'You look a knockout,' I told her when she reached the bottom.

'Thank you, kind sir,' said she.

Mrs did not feel like talking much, so we ate our food in silence. There was no dessert, so I made Mrs some coffee from a percolator on the sideboard.

'Tell me,' she said, 'what do you think about your life? I mean, is it going the way you thought it would?' She coiled her fingers round a strand of her long black hair and looked down at the floor.

'I don't think about it much,' I replied.

'Don't you have any goals in life – any dreams – any projects?'

'I'd like to go away on holiday sometime.'

'Where would you like to go?' she asked animatedly. 'Tahiti? Fiji? The Galagapos?

'I was thinking of somewhere closer to home. Clacton. Or Devon.'

This made her laugh, so much so that I ended up clapping her on the back to make her stop.

'Oh come on. You can't be serious'

'I haven't the money to go to such out-of-the-way places,' I said.

'I'll take you!' she suddenly said, her eyes wide and black. Then the excitement dissipated. She slouched in her chair, her face listless and shapeless, like a badly kneaded piece of dough.

'Come on!' I said. 'It's not as bad as all that.'

'If only life were simple,' she said. 'But he could find me anywhere. Anywhere in the world.'

'Mine is!' I volunteered, and this, for some reason, made her laugh. This time she had the hiccups, so she stopped. Mrs Craddock brought coffee for both of us, and we drank it in silence.

Later, in the living room, we played some records, some old Procul Harum – *A Whiter Shade of Pale*. I held her close to me and did a slow shuffling dance. She seemed to enjoy it. We polished off half a bottle of whisky between us. And then we went to bed.

I woke to find the muzzle tip of a shotgun in my mouth. It tasted of metal and oil. Mrs was asleep beside me. The unshaven and beetroot face of Pharaoh bore down upon me. I thought it was beetroot because at that time it must have looked more green than red because of the glow of the night-sights goggles he was wearing.

'Prick!' he murmured.

To judge by the way the tip of the shotgun was rattling my teeth I knew it was not a good idea to agitate him. I stayed as still as possible. His breath was rank and was coming fast. I looked along the length of the gun and saw his trigger finger was tensed in a menacing fashion. But he did not fire. Instead I took advantage of a momentary hesitation on his part, to push the gun away from my mouth with my free hand and fall out of bed. I and the gun clattered to the ground but mercifully the gun did not go off. I had no time to grab it as I reckoned the best thing to do was dart past Pharaoh and out of the room as fast as possible. All I succeeded in doing was running into the arms of three men who had obviously been waiting for me, hands at the ready. They were hefty buggers too, dressed in security detail, black suits and army haircuts. After one wheeled off to help a panting Ahmed to his feet, the other two escorted me downstairs to the pantry and locked me in. Then I heard a couple of thuds, followed by screams, moans, and then silence. I didn't try to escape or cry for help. One of the security men let me out and said it would be a good idea if I left now. Finding myself outside in the cold air, I climbed into the Mercedes and started it up. I always kept the keys in the sun visor, in best Hollywood fashion. I drove back to London. In the morning I went and looked for work.

I understand Ahmed and Mrs got divorced. It was very messy and in all the papers. She petitioned him on the grounds of adultery and creamed fifty million. I got my old job back in the baths. Although free, Mrs never came to look me up nor did she phone. I was not even cited in the divorce. According to the papers, the fault lay entirely with Pharaoh. He married his girlfriend. I wrote to her a few times but never received a reply. I have just sold the Mercedes for £10,000. I'll spend the money on going round the world. I intend now to widen my circle of friends. I have a good body and am not bad looking. A number of openings are available to me. I could be a male escort or a general handyman. I'll sort it out when I get home.

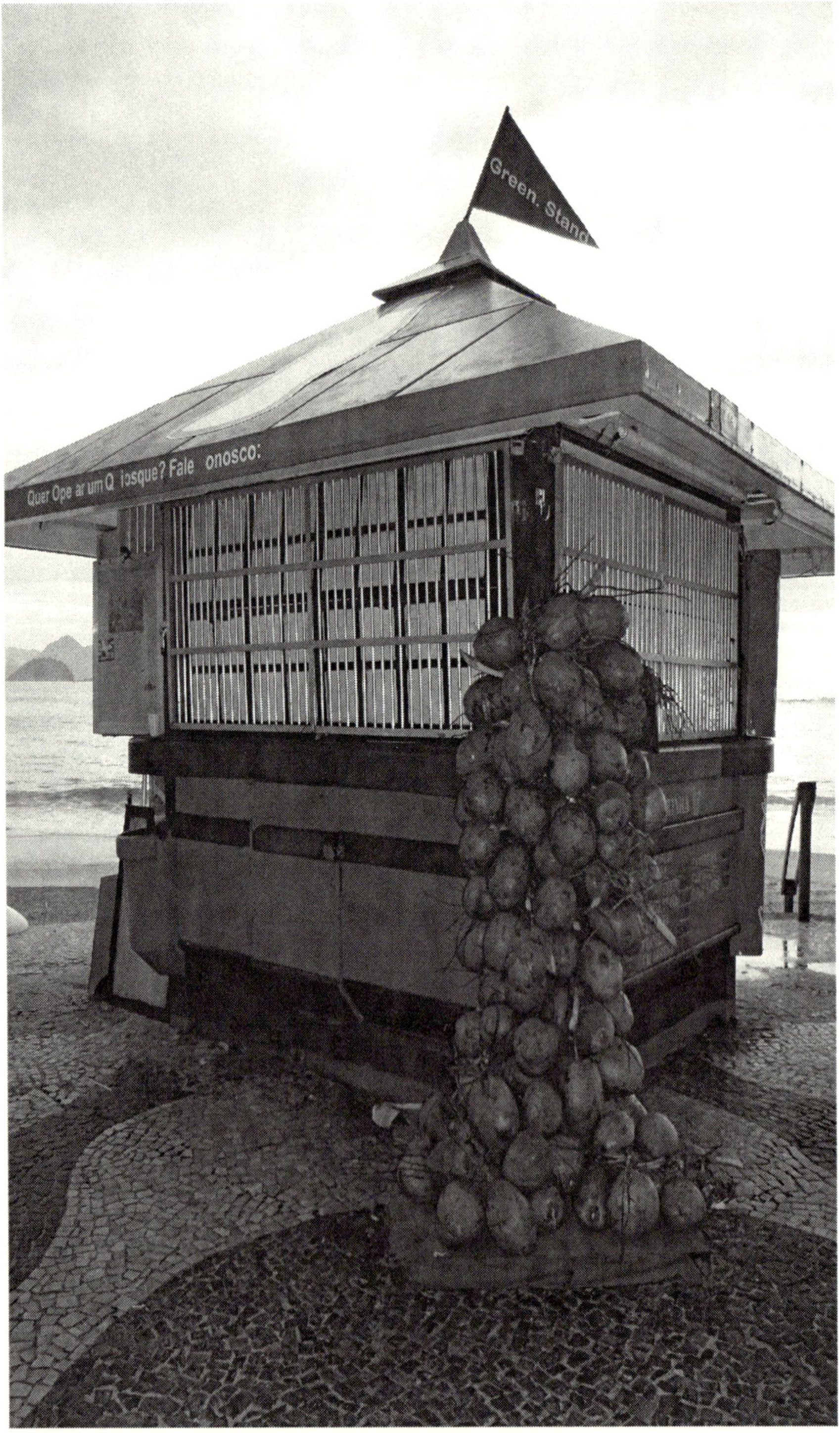
Green. Stand
Quer Ope ar um Q iosque? Fale onosco:

BOATMAN

You can recognise us pretty easily around the world, I guess. We're tanned from the outdoors, wear tee shirts and cut-off jeans and, most of all, possess a kind of loucheness that comes from being free from a nine-to-five routine. We're drifters, losers, chancers, escaped, released, or paroled prisoners, travellers, and suspects of unsolved crimes. You can include me in the latter category.

As I took the ferry from Dover the phrase 'England killed me' kept going round in my mind. My confidence grew the further I got away from the shore. The past literally seemed another country; all my actions seemed bound up in complications. It was only necessary to cut the Gordian knot to escape.

I had no real idea where I was going and had only £500 in my pocket. I carried only a small rucksack; it was the best way to be. I was twenty-nine years old. I was leaving behind a mess; I knew that. What

I did not know was that you can escape but the past will always find a way of striking back.

But then I didn't care. I made my way from France to Spain and from Spain, just for the kicks, I went to Ibiza and then, as the summer season was getting going, to Majorca. I didn't much like it there. I didn't like being round my own kind. I mean English people. And Majorca is stuffed with them. So I made my way to Minorca, which was similarly stuffed, but gentler on the senses.

I found my way to the pretty harbour town of Mahon and needed to look for work. What skills did I have? A half-finished university education was hardly likely to recommend me to a professional career. And then I discovered boats. You couldn't be in Mahon without finding them. There are stacks of them, all ranged on pontoons throughout the five-mile harbour. The good thing about the boats in Minorca is, like any place with a high ex-pat population, they need attention while the owners are absent. When they return for their one- or -two week 'holiday' in which they've invested thousands, they find, horror of horrors, that the vessels for which they have paid a sum equivalent to a house mortgage, present 'problems.' The engines that were supposed to have been turned are rock solid; cabins are mysteriously flooded ('The pump broke, sir'). It's called *guardinage,* which is another word for extracting money by degrees from well-heeled but technically ignorant clients. And it is all perfectly legal. For example, a pump breaks down, it's replaced with a second-hand one charged as new; a battery needs replacing? Chuck in a cheap low grade one but charge a high price spec. I fell in with one of these companies and pretty soon became adept at padding time sheets while for the most part ignoring the vessels I was supposed to maintain on a regular basis.

Towards the end of the season I got bored. Travelling up to the coastal town of Addaya one weekend I found a boat I rather liked and decided to learn sailing by experience. It wasn't difficult to open the hatch, start her up, and head due east. If you head in that direction in the Mediterranean for long enough, you are bound to hit something. After about 200 miles in hairy weather (chart information: 'Beware *mistral* wind which kicks up short sharp waves') I spied land. It was nightfall when I dropped anchor and fell asleep almost immediately. When I woke, at first light, I found I had drifted into the centre of a large bay, and, on making enquiries with locals, discovered I was in Sardinia. What country, friends, is this? This is Illyria, lady. Illyria? It might have been, for aught I knew.

I was in a quiet part of the island, and I was not even required to check into customs or anything like that. I made my way to a small marina and moored with a local fishing boat on one side and a forty-foot sloop on the other. Well, boats attract eccentrics and losers.... Have I made myself clear? The family that lived on the boat next to mine were no exception, nor were the owners of the boat yard, who consisted of a giant of a mechanic and his boss, a tough, grizzled fifty-five-year-old, Sergio. Everything was antiquated and ramshackle and, best of all, no one except Sergio spoke English. Now I was truly in a foreign land. The people who lived on the boat next to mine were French.

I first got to know them when I spotted something wrong with their boat and offered to help. In boat world, you are judged first by the boat you have and then by your practical prowess. It wasn't difficult, peering through the transparent water, to see that there was a rope caught round his prop. I offered to go in and cut it. Waving aside his objections that the water was too cold and too deep, I dove in and with my knife had the rope detached in no time. Of course he invited me on to his boat for a quick hose down, in 'hot water, run off the engine.' Owners are inordinately proud of their boats even when they are heaps. His engine burned oil, his interior was ragged, and his wife looked haggard. He had a teenage daughter, a sallow-faced placid thing. They amused themselves by playing cards all day and going nowhere. This is called floating caravan syndrome. The more you stay tied up in the dock, the more afraid you are to go out because you are always tending to something that is wrong. Any self-respecting sailor would have dived down and cut the rope from the prop. But Paul (he told me his name – I did not tell him mine) was 'waiting for the diver.' Paul was sixty and had a bad back, he told me. And no, the woman he introduced me to and who looked traumatised by the Spartan experience of boat living, was a 'friend,' not his wife.

Later, after showing me his engine (75 Hp, 'old but in good order' – who is he kidding?), he admitted the boat was for sale – note, every boat is for sale.

Later still, when I was gossiping in the yard, Sergio told me the man's sorry tale. Paul had arrived with his wife three years ago in the teeth of a howling storm. He knew nothing about boats, and the wife was terrified. He couldn't even moor the boat. When they were safely ashore, the wife fled back to Switzerland leaving him an ultimatum: choose me or the boat. Boats and women rarely mix. In any case Paul kept the boat, lost the wife, and mouldered in the port ever since. Now he had found a fresh victim but had not set sail again.

After I returned to 'my boat' to do some running repairs, I had him over to inspect my quarters. He remarked how superb my boat was and suggested we do some sailing in tandem. He suggested some destinations. We chose one and decided to set out the next day. I was in any case eager to be off. But the next morning he popped his head up through the hatch of his boat and said, 'Bad weather, we better not go today.'

I looked across at a mirror-like sea and replied, 'No, you shall eat your soup today!' 'No, no,' he protested, 'I have heard a weather forecast.'

I knew he was one of those people who always procrastinate, so I insisted and at last he relented. I helped him get underway, and we had a very pleasant motor sail on a placid sea without a cloud in the sky. We rounded the *cabo* at the end of the bay and headed for some ruins at Tharros some 100 miles south.

It was then that everything started to go wrong. I had had a good run of it, so I suppose I shouldn't complain. Anyway, as we approached the coast it was apparent that news of my activities in Minorca had reached Sardinia as I could see through my binoculars a heavy contingent of *carabineri* on the dock side. As we were sailing in close order, it was not difficult to bring my boat alongside on the pretext that I needed help and hailed Paul to jump over to me and give the helm to his female friend for a few seconds. He did so reluctantly but gamely. No sooner had he done so that I jumped across to his boat, shoved the woman from the wheel, and moved the morse control to full throttle, which caused to boat to bank sharply, change direction, and leave Paul heading for the coast while I, his friend, and the teenage girl headed to open sea. Within a few seconds the distance soon drowned out his cries. The woman protested and gesticulated, but I ignored her. She tried to wrench the wheel from me, but a strong wave broadside soon put paid to that. She gave up and sat there glowering at me before going below. I had the sense to follow her and cut the radio cable as she was picking up the mike. The girl, who had never appeared on deck, just looked at me. The woman stared but there was nothing they could do. The engine on Paul's boat was far more powerful than mine, and he must have realised there was no way he could catch me. He had obviously thought it more sensible to head for the quayside.

The wind was really getting up now and the swell was such that when the boat crested it was like looking downstairs from the top landing. Once in a while the distance from boat to the wave trough was such that it felt like looking down from the roof of a house. We had lost sight of Paul completely. The dreaded north wind started to kick up the sea into shorter ridges with breaking crests of white foam and stinging spray. The boat was ploughing through it all, but if it got any worse, there would be nothing for it but to let her run with the wind. I heard nothing from the two women because they were suffering from *mal de mer* and within a few hours there was no one but me at the helm, that and the wind, and the raging sea.

For a while I enjoyed it. Then when I thought the wind could not blow any stronger, it redoubled its strength and soon I was wishing I had stayed on my boat and given myself up. We were running before the storm almost due south, and if it kept up like this we would be in Tunisia in a couple of days! That would be a good thing. I would be outside European jurisdiction and home, free. Meanwhile the wind screamed in the rigging, and the boat's belly bounced over the waves, sometimes digging her bow deep into a trough, at other times taking some water over the stern. Still I had the engine at low revs, and this helped me point up to avoid a nasty breaker. But when a large wave broke on board, it gave up and the batteries flooded. It was soon too dangerous for me to remain in the cockpit. I lashed the wheel and joined the women below, bolting the hatch from inside. Life below was not improved by the fetid atmosphere, made all the worse by the poisonous glances aimed at me by my green-faced crew. The girl, in particular, lay moaning on a bunk, unresisting even while the violent motion of the boat threw her from one side to the other. The elder woman simply curled up and wedged herself on the cabin sole between the two bunks. I crouched down by the chart table and waited for the storm to abate.

Sixteen hours later, the motion of the boat perceptibly eased, but we were too tired to care. Half dozing, sick, damp from the water creeping down the hatch from above, bruised from objects that had hurled themselves from their lockers, all we could do was drag ourselves up for a look at the sea. At early light there was still a mighty swell, but the crests were not being whipped from the top of the waves. It was containable. We were not going to drown.

I left the females below to recover and clear up while I checked the boat. The furling genoa was in a sorry state, blown to ribbons. The main sail was still OK, and we could make land under sail alone. I had no idea where we were but the GPS told me we were fifteen miles from the Sicilian coast.

I went below and found they were just sitting there staring at me, like cubs found in a set by a hunt dog. I thought I might get angry, but suppressed it, and just tidied stuff up the best I could and sorted out some dry rations. Normally on a boat I don't get that hungry when sailing, but now I needed something warm inside me. The problem was the woman was uncooperative. She might not have known English, but she made her displeasure known by the way she bored into me with her accusatory stare. All I needed was a moody bitch on board. The girl on the other hand was passivity personified. She did absolutely nothing except look at herself in a small mirror and straighten her hair. I suspected there was something wrong with her. She seemed so remote from what was going on. I realised I had to somehow get the older woman on my side. So when she came up on deck for some air, I said, 'You know, Paul wanted my boat. He preferred it.'

I don't know if she believed me or not but she looked my way and then it wasn't difficult to ask her to look up at the sail while I gave her a push from behind. She went into the water without a sound, almost as if she was expecting it. Perhaps she didn't care. The job done, I went below and tidied up. The girl said nothing. She just looked at me. I suddenly felt very tired and in need of warmth. It seemed the most natural thing to go to her and cuddle. She placed her thin white arms loosely on my back and let me nuzzle up. Pretty soon I found myself making love to her. I unleashed all my being on her in a miniature human version of the storm we had just endured. But again she made hardly a sound.

Later, as the sea flattened out, I felt a thousand times better. I was looking straight ahead and did not hear or notice the patrol RIB approach from the stern and board my boat. But instead of arresting me I found the mustachioed *carabinieri* officers looked relieved, even cheerful.

'Thanks to you,' the officer in charge told me after a brief greeting, 'we have caught him.'

I thought it politic to break open a bottle of brandy that astonishingly had not been used during that voyage, and I handed tots round to the three officers on deck. This gesture certainly did the trick. The officer in charge became garrulous.

'Did you know he had killed his wife?' he asked me. They looked around the boat. 'There was another woman here also, wasn't there?' I nodded. 'He put paid to her and escaped. Very clever,' said the officer. 'And the young girl?' he asked. 'Wasn't there a girl also on board?' I nodded and shrugged. The girl emerged from below. The officer smiled at her. 'You had a lucky escape,' he told her. As usual, she neither smiled nor replied. That was her way, I guess.

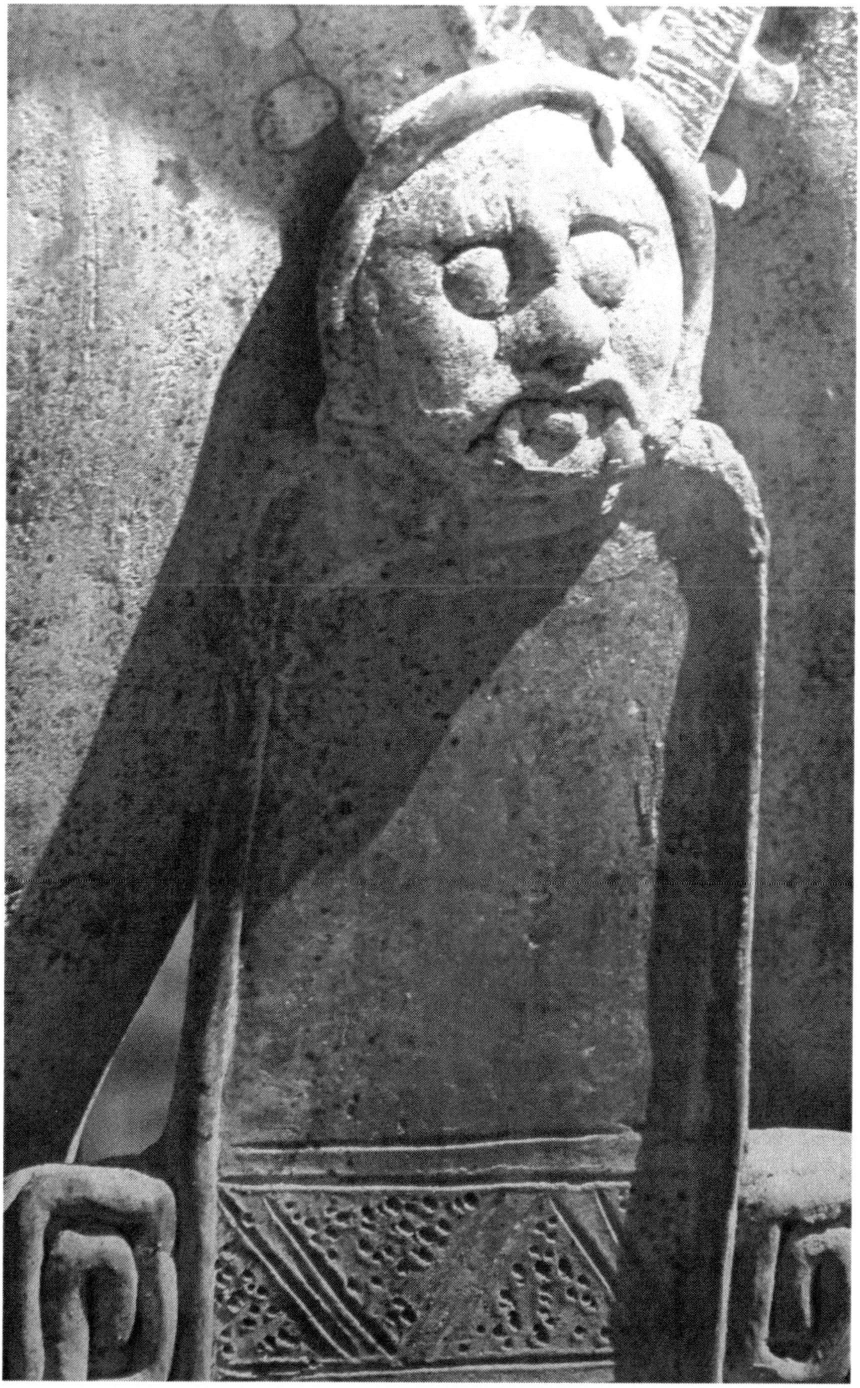

ONE FOR THE ROAD

I have to admit I viewed John Gegen's *Exhibition of Nothing* in the same way I did the front cover of the book, *Does My Bum Look Big In This?*, that is, with a sneer of the lip, Elvis style, my contempt growing only with the success of both artists. And if, as some critics say, the function of art is to provoke, then both succeed. But of course, how can that be the only criterion? Only in a new barbaric age, an age of *feuilleton*, as Hermann Hesse puts it, can such a state of affairs persist against the grain of common sense.

John Gegen's art received its accolade at the Tate Modern, where he was celebrated as the chief exponent of conceptual art. He was, said one critic, at the zenith of the movement, sitting at the apex of its development. After Gegen (or Gaga as John preferred to be called) there was nowhere else for art to go; 'Gaga has sealed off all the exits; from now on all one can do is sit open-mouthed in admiration.'

Open-mouthed several of us were, but in my case it was from sheer admiration at the effrontery of the man. How in God's name did he imagine he would get away with it? Yet he did, and, indeed, because I had known him since childhood this was doubtless why he confided in me on the first day of the exhibition. He approached me, glass of wine in hand and said, 'Of course, Eric, you do realise that if I had my way there would be nothing here at all. Nothing at all. But you see,' he went on, sitting down next to me on the bench and patting my knee, 'The collectors, you see, they have to have something to take away with them.'

'All they've got are frames,' I said, gesturing feebly to a rectangle gently moving out from the wall against which it was suspended in time to the circulation of the gallery's air conditioning. 'And don't tell me the guff about being able to project whatever I want on to the wall behind the frames. I can see through it all,' I added, cruelly.

'I shall ignore the crudity of your statement,' he said. 'I should have so loved the purity that would have gone with having an entirely empty gallery, devoid of any product whatsoever. But we are corrupted by the need to possess, without which I am the first to admit, I would be deprived of the wherewithal with which I sustain my decadent lifestyle, chiefly in relation to the obtaining and retention of quantities of women, wine, and fags.'

David Del Monté

On the drive home afterwards, I reflected upon John's words. As I was negotiating the traffic, a metaphor for what John had said rose in my mind. It was only because it was generally agreed that John was an artist and that the frames were art that made them so. He was fashionable, of course, and had a lifestyle and PR machine that went with all that. The whole thing was like the traffic. It is agreed, tacitly, that everyone may act in a way in public that privately everyone shies away from, unless mentally deranged. I mean, if you were to lock yourself in your garage and start the engine, it would only be a few minutes before you would be dead from carbon monoxide poisoning. However, in their adverts in colour magazines, car manufacturers hardly extol the beauty of gassing their fellow citizens. Usually such adverts display a solitary driver at the wheel of his vehicle in command of a stretch of lonely country road either in the highlands of Scotland or somewhere on the Cote d'Azur. But that is not all. There is complicity about the whole business of traffic. We're all part of the conspiracy of death. This permissive state of affairs, in which I am both the victim (the inhaler of your fumes), and the oppressor (the exhaler of dangerous chemicals), puts all of us using cars in a silent pact. We allow each other to poison each other so that we can drive. On top of having the right to poison you I will affirm the high level of my culture by adopting good driving practices. I shall flash my lights to let you go, and I will pass you when it is safe, and even smile at appropriate moments. You, on the other hand, agree not to crash into me when driving towards me from the opposite direction. I will be kind even as I am killing you. Only duelling in the last century displayed such a paradox of civilisation. Should mankind survive, posterity will laugh at the hypocrisy of our claims to be civilised.

I wish to God I had not communicated some of these thoughts to Gaga when he called me on my mobile for reassurance. For a major artist who had, I would have thought, enough media attention to ensure his validation, he was quite insecure (not without good reason as he was totally lacking in talent. But I played the hypocrite well enough and praised him to the skies when he rang, and, as a coda, rattled on about my theory.

He did not sound interested at the time, but I should have known his mind was racing as I spoke, galloping ahead to the next phase in his life, searching always to the next opportunity that would present itself, anticipating as any opportunist would, the time when the art scam might fall away, and seeking always to keep his name in the spotlight. This could only be achieved by more innovations or by running in another direction entirely.

I did not appreciate the extent of his political connections until, at a press conference a month after I had spoken to him, Gaga and the then mayor of London announced their traffic initiative. It seems extraordinary now when I think of it, but you have to cast your mind back to the fevered atmosphere of those times. The roads were almost grid-locked; the mayor needed an initiative to kick-start his re-election campaign; Gaga too needed an impetus since a career in art, founded on sensation, could only survive by harnessing itself to an ascendant scale on which a series of increasingly extreme notes would be played.

Traffic signs provided the means by which both politician and artist could achieve their goals. Presented in huge letters on an elaborate projection behind them were the words TRAFFIC KINDNESS. The reality was anything but; in the newspeak of the times, and with the right media spin, it would not be difficult, they imagined, bringing public opinion on to their side.

'The time for voluntary restraint is over,' the mayor said, with Gaga nodding beside him. 'Our research shows that ninety per cent of car journeys are totally unnecessary. For too long we have permitted the driver to clog up our streets. Now he will be invited to share his vehicle with others. Vehicle sharing,' the mayor continued, 'will be promoted as a policy when camera monitors, installed above the road, detect a car containing only one occupant. A flash from the camera's strobe light will give the driver the opportunity to stop his vehicle and get out. If he fails to do so, police will be given the power to stop the vehicle and arrest the driver. Drivers in cars containing two or more occupants will be allowed by the cameras to go about their business.'

It all sounded eminently reasonable at the time and was applauded as a great initiative. The mayor was re-elected with an increased majority on the basis of his new 'transport policy.' Meanwhile, Gaga cosied up even more to the political faction in which the mayor featured prominently. All seemed to go wrong when it became obvious that drivers were ignoring the cameras' flashes and the police did not have the manpower to stop infringers. Soon the mayor's vaunted policy was in shreds; it was simply ignored and the selfish driver went about his business of poisoning his fellow citizens in time-honoured fashion. Something more drastic was called for and Gaga supplied it.

'Cull them,' he advised.

This was too much for the mayor.

'Come on, John,' he is reported to have said, 'I'm not a mass murderer!'

John laughed.

'Not the drivers. The cars. Cull the cars.'

'Cull the cars? Mmm.'

The mayor stroked his chin and thought about it.

'How?'

It was at this point that John produced his *coup de theatre*.

'My friends at the ministry of defence,' he said, hauling up an enormous bazooka type object, 'have given me this for demonstration purposes only. It discharges a magnetic pulse which, when aimed at a car, will demobilise it instantly.'

'I like it!' said the mayor. 'Cars culled in mayoral purge!' he said excitedly, anticipating the headlines that would surely be his. 'We must pilot this right away.'

After some delay caused by inter-departmental squabbles and objections by the road transport lobby, the mayor's initiative went into service. Now the strobe flashes were discontinued in favour of the new weapon. Before long its deterrent value had proved itself. None wanted to wait for hours for a mechanic to re-activate their vehicles. Car sharing became de rigueur. It seemed as if the mayor's plan had worked. Traffic kindness had become the norm. But the politician had underestimated people's ingenuity. Before he had the chance to reap the political dividends in vote-catching headlines, a dose of cold reality set in. Cars, which looked full, contained in reality life-like dummies. The mayor retaliated by equipping sensors with heat-seeking devices; the drivers retaliated by installing warmers inside their inflatable dolls; the mayor hit back by installing heartbeat sensors inside the roadside monitors; the drivers returned fire by inserting mechanical hearts torn from toy teddies until, exasperated and on the verge of becoming a laughing stock, the mayor turned to Gaga for salvation.

'The whole business is a mess,' he said. 'I wished I had never listened to you. I will be hauled up before the audit commission and be accused of wasting millions of public funds on a device that doesn't work. What will deter these bloody drivers, for God's sake?'

John passed the mayor a stiff whisky and ginger, and smiled.

'I've thought of a way,' he said. 'Erect toll booths where drivers and their passengers will have to give a sample of saliva. That way every occupant of a car will have his or her DNA tested. Now show me,' he asked, 'an inflatable dummy that can prove it's human?'

The mayor left his drink untouched, pale with exhaustion, an expression of horror on his face. He blamed himself for having tangled with the art world.

'Are you mad?' he asked.

John nodded sagely.

'No, you're right,' he said. 'They will probably get round that one too. There's no way escaping it. You will have to cull the drivers.'

The mayor watched as John downed his drink.

'It's the only way. Look at it as humanitarian. Of course you needn't do it deliberately. Just say one of the guns went wrong. Instead of emitting a magnetic pulse – useless! – get one that detonates a neutron bomb in the precise direction of the offending vehicle. That would kill the driver without harming the car. I know someone who can adapt them. For a price. Call it an accident. I bet it will thin out the traffic. Just repeat the 'accident' at intervals during the year and watch the effect. It will be dramatic. It will be like a lottery. Nobody will know if it could be them. People will know it's the mayor's policy. There will be a tacit but non-verbal conspiracy of acknowledgement that you're right. For drastic measures have to be taken. People won't like to admit it but they will agree you had no other choice. But you'll call it an accident, though it won't be. Everyone will know those drivers died as sacrifices and examples to others. Give them a good funeral, pay some compensation, hold an enquiry, and then do it again. Give the brief to a colleague you want to get rid of, then do it again. It's like driving. My friend Eric told me. We agree to let us murder each other by poisoning the planet. We all do it. We carry on doing it because we want to drive. This way you'll put a stop to driving for all but the bravest or most foolish. Drive everyone on to public transport. You'll be re-elected until you're gaga.' He laughed at the pun on his own name.

The mayor stroked his chin and listened. This time he took a sip from his drink. He enjoyed the weighty feel of the cut crystal. Life was good up there in the penthouse restaurant he had built with public money. He did not want all that to end. He wanted to be prime minister one day. Who was to say he could not achieve that? He was amazed and pleased by his friend's profound grasp of political reality.

'What you are suggesting,' the mayor said, with a hark back to his days as a radical, 'is a campaign of terror.'

'That's about the long and short of it,' said John.

The mayor bent his head close to John's.

'Do it,' he said.

It went according to plan, and the mayor gained the political kudos that resulted. People were driven from their cars but were too embarrassed to admit it. To drive was to be, ipso facto, selfish. When the first victim died, it was discovered he was alone in his car in contravention of the rules. The mayor's PR machine swung into action. The man was white, middle-aged, and bald. He was divorced and drank to excess. Rumour had it he beat his wife. He was a furniture salesman on his way to an appointment. The police found a small attaché case with samples inside the car. He could have taken that attaché case on the tube! Ergo, it was his own fault he got zapped. Soon the tabloids got the gist of the game. An out-of-towner from the north, not realising how lethal the capital's streets had become, had his demise celebrated in the Sun by the headline: GOTCHA! It had the echo of an atrocity which had been presented previously in similarly entertaining terms. Two German tourists were zapped two months later, but this was hushed up and soon deaths occurred at fairly regular intervals without much public comment. The novelty of the story had worn off, and the policy was successful. The streets were all but empty.

For John, however, the plaudits did not rain down as they did on the head of the now celebrated mayor of London. John, having believed his own propaganda and convinced he was the greatest artist of the twenty-first century, found it hard to endure the years of neglect that quickly followed his *Exhibition of Nothing*. He wrote a book in which he claimed the credit for the mayor's road policy. He was pooh-poohed as a fantasist, and when I saw him he was angry. His hollow eyes and unshaven appearance gave me an impression that he was on the slide in a big way. But John was not finished yet.

'I'll show them,' he told me over his cups, and I thought, like everyone, that this was an idle threat made by a feeble, prematurely middle-aged man who was now ignored by everyone who mattered. Gone were the swaggering, the huge fees, and the stunts.

Yet John had one stunt yet to pull.

On the evening of 22 June last year, as the mayor was climbing into his chauffeur-driven car on his way to a function, a man was seen brandishing a bazooka-shaped object. It apparently had been stolen, with professional help, from its mount above the Archway Road in North London.

Swaggering and the worse for wear the artist claimed he was going to destroy the mayor and anyone else who got in his way. The army was called, and the man was seen swaying up the Embankment by the Thames, holding this enormous weapon, a couple of loose wires trailing out the back. A police SWAT team, supported by a helicopter, followed the criminal as he described his crazy route and the area was cleared of traffic (hardly difficult in any case). It soon became clear that John's destination was the houses of parliament and the SWAT teams indicated that they were prepared to take him out at any time. They only needed word from the mayor.

That word never came. John was allowed to walk the entire length of the Embankment and it seemed, was being encouraged, albeit tacitly, to discharge his weapon in the direction of the assembled legislature.

'No,' John was heard to shout, 'I won't do it. Not to further your career, Mr Mayor! How many have died to achieve that?'

His comments were recorded and transmitted later on the television news. Much to the mayor's chagrin, it was alleged, a brave officer body-charged John and brought him down. The mayor did not want any charges brought against John, but the story came out through the activities of investigative journalists who had been blind to the obvious only a few months previously. The mayor was getting too big for his boots. His inactivity over the 'Neutron Affair' was labelled complicity and this, the prime minister stated, could never be allowed.

The weapons were removed and within two days, almost like a miracle, the traffic in the capital resumed its previous levels. The great experiment was over. The mayor was arrested for murder, and the entire London council for corporate manslaughter. At his trial the mayor defended his policy as being for the 'public good.' This defence was roundly rejected by the prosecuting counsel. However, against all the odds the mayor's luck held, and he was acquitted by a jury sympathetic to his extreme but clearly effective polices, thus showing that voters like their politicians to be crueller than kind.

John himself is serving five years in Ford Open Prison. Sometimes I visit him there and talk of old times. We never talk about cars. It is just too painful.

People are just as polite as they used to be on the road, which is nice. Others drive peering about as if in a war zone, unsure if they might be picked off and unable to believe what they hear about it being safe to go out once more. It is said that due to the irresponsible actions of some drivers who are reacting to their new-found freedom by driving with abandon, some drastic action might need to be taken. But like a war-weary population no one really has the stomach for it. We all feel a little bit guilty at what went on, truth to tell. About having allowed it to happen. Perhaps it is safer for us to die of monoxide poisoning after all. Others say it is best to leave it to the mayor. He'll come up with a solution. He always does.

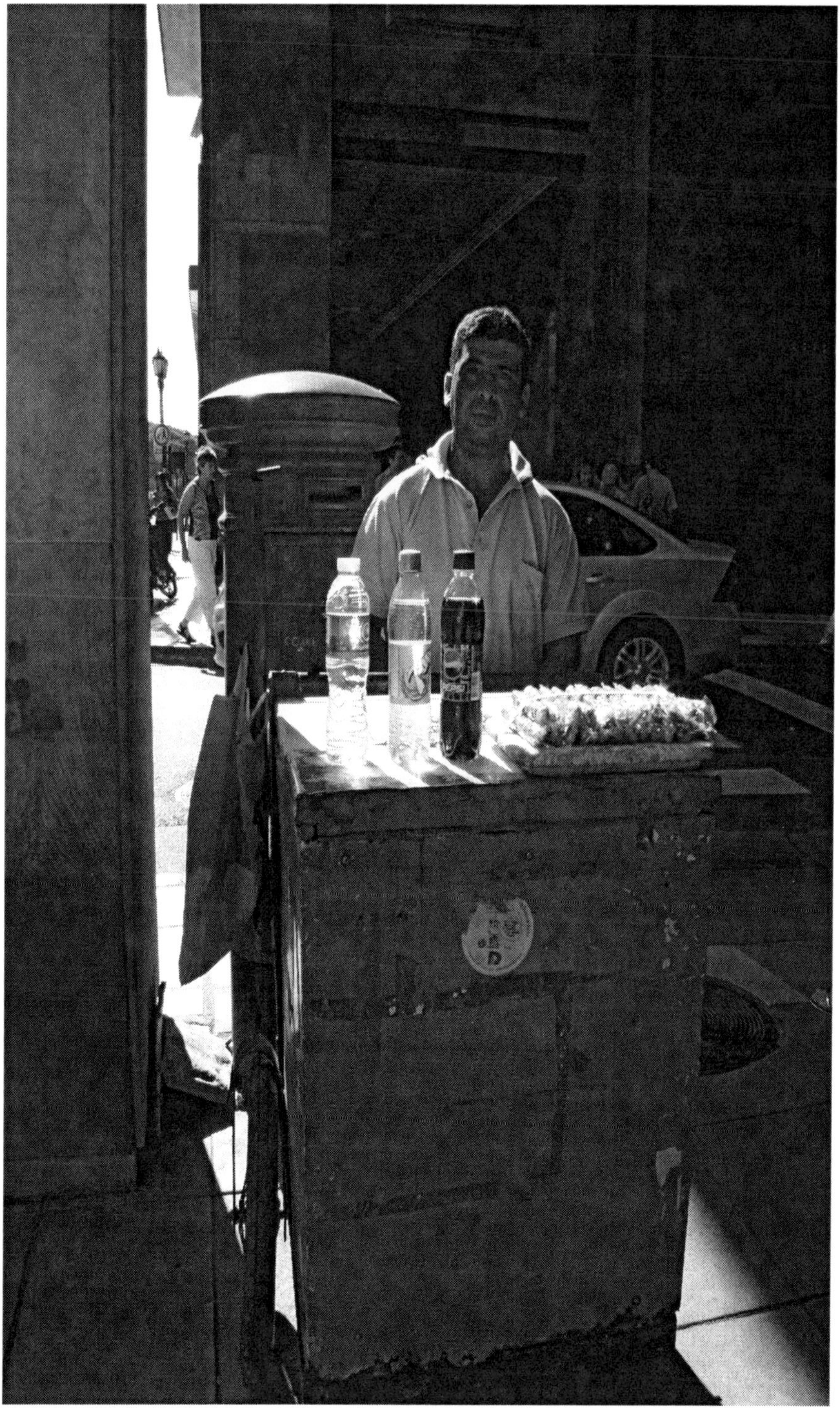

THE SWITCH

It was in the year 1605 that our sovereign King James I granted me, Captain Stephen Stephens, the opportunity, with 234 other souls, to voyage to the New World and there make a colony. I need not rehearse the rigours of that voyage or the first season in which our two hundred reduced to two score; the history is well known. Disease, starvation, and Indian attack all played their parts in reducing our number, and truly, we were a sorry band that endured into the second year. Sir Walter Raleigh had assured us that potato is a staple that can sustain a man. I can tell him that the vegetable is insufficient to sustain a man solely; other nutrients are required, chiefly fish. We are nought but chips off the old block, I wrote. In his reply, Sir Walter told that parings would suffice us in the second and third years; in other words, we would live upon chips and fish.

We brought with us a few wenches for breeding stock, and I can well remember the shrieks of joy these women raised as we espied land that first year. They all died, alas, but one, and she was my Fair One, who gave birth to a son in the year 1607, may the Lord be praised. Thank God she lived long enough to see his cherubic face and after that expired. There was nothing for me to do but call upon the services of an Indian squaw, as they are termed, to nurse my little one.

This I was hard put to achieve, since the Indians, although less hostile than they had been previously, having seen our number decrease so substantially, were now hardly disposed to see an increase in the white race which, in their eyes, had impinged upon their territory. Nonetheless, the sight of my poor little one mewling excited the sympathies of the tribe. In my best doublet and bearing gifts of glass and two daggers, I prostrated myself before their chief and presented my baby, clasping him close as the braves approached, spears in hand. I was sure they would pierce my baby's neck, and then mine, and thereupon end all our hopes, but instead the chief stared at the infant, and then commanded him be brought to where he sat king-like on a rock. There the chief of the Indians stared and stared at my boy and then, with calloused, rough, and dark fingers, he began to prod gently at his coverings and opened them up. He made a sound in curiosity and wonderment as my little one's fair skin was revealed. At his touch, my son ceased crying and relaxed as the chief removed all his garments.

David Del Monté

Then, making his right hand into a hook, he summoned several of his women to attend upon him. Three squaws approached, and he spoke to them in a guttural way, making odd popping sounds. These women took up my boy and went off with him. I was at least relieved that he lived and that I too was alive to look upon the world a while longer. I rose, but the chief peremptorily ordered me to remain kneeling, which I did. A few minutes later one of the women came back bearing a bundle. She cradled an infant Indian boy and put him in my arms. I was to understand I was to take him as my own son, in lieu of the boy I had given up. This boy, although weaned, was sickly, and, I thought, would not live long. It was clearly not an exchange favourable to me, but I could do nothing but take him away, accompanied by a whole number of whooping braves, who took me back to the edge of our camp and there departed with salutations.

Thereafter we had no further problems with the Indians. Attacks ceased and our colony was allowed to prosper and continue, although, of course, without breeding stock. We were destined to perish there upon Virginia's shores unless we could be replenished from England, an unlikely instance when all knew in our fair land that our women had died and this was hardly a great advertisement to attract fresh stock. My Indian boy, whom I could not call Stephen after our family tradition (or want of imagination, call it what you will and in any case it was the name of the son I had so sadly given away), I called Indy, and this appellation was accepted well enough, except that for almost two days this Indian boy sat and wailed and tried to escape between the wooden piles in our stockade until we forcibly tied him down, thinking that, as he was likely to die, such torture would not long detain him. God, in His mercy decided otherwise, and, despite the paucity of food, he survived, although bent and scrawny, and soon was accepting of us, and running about the camp like any child. At first he was abused and hated by the men. He endured their blows only because he was considered our enemy. But soon he became a sort of mascot. He was the only young thing there and he reminded the men of their own lack of progeny and of home. And so he was, by degrees, tolerated and later, I would even say, loved. Of course it was hardly six months before Indy forgot most or all of his Indian ways and adopted ours. By the same token, I knew well that my boy Stephen, brought up in the Indian camp, would become foreign. To my content, I observed this oft enough during the summer months over the next years, when I visited the Indian village to trade and to see my boy. I was not permitted any private audience, and it was clear that when a ragged band of Indian boys scampered around my legs, that my boy, white and taller than his mates, did not recognise me as his father but only as a stranger, white and blue-eyed though he was.

And so it was and so it went on for five more years, until 1610 when we were finally re-supplied with weapons, colonists, foodstuffs,

David Del Monté

and above all, fresh females, as well as one pastor. The moment they landed, the men fell upon the women as famished beasts, having been deprived of female company for so long and sorely distressed for that reason. I chose for myself one fair girl called Nell, who was, until lately, my second wife.

On the day after festivities and a feast, the pastor, his name was Abraham Abrahams (after a family tradition similar to mine), sought me out and sat down with me by the root of an old oak tree.

'Tell me, Mr Stephens,' said he, 'The meaning of that boy of yours, Indy, whom I see, is part of our company?'

I told him the story of the switch forced upon me by circumstance, the death of my first wife, and the need to preserve the life of my son.

'It is strange, is it not, that you made no mention of this incident in your dispatches?'

'We had other more pressing matters than my affairs,' I replied.

'Yet surely,' said the pastor, 'the presence of a savage amongst us is an abomination.'

I stood up.

'An abomination?'

He rose and hastily tapped me upon the shoulder.

'Perhaps I phrase myself too harshly. I forgot that you must have come to love the Indian boy whereas I see only... well, an animal, shall I say? For want of a better word. Now, don't be angry, Mr Stephens.

All I am saying is that if you want your own boy back, we now have the power to help you. Don't you understand? With our new weaponry and the company, we can force our will upon the heathens and make another switch, this time of our liking. What do you say?'

I stood astonished and knew not what to say. It was a matter best brought up in a general camp meeting. The old timers, like myself, were few in number but were subdued by the clamours of the newcomers who did not know the local ways and were for war and supremacy in that area. They saw from afar the smoke of the Indian village; they saw too their multitude of animals. They said it was only a matter of time before the winter came and then we would have to choose between attack by the Indians and resultant extermination or survival, triumph, and supremacy.

I told the company that for about four years there had been no Indian attack and although amity had not led to mixing and marrying as yet (an angry cry went up when I said this), one man, Edward Perkins, had said he would better have married an Indian woman rather than leave no issue upon the Earth. Nonetheless, my counsel did not prevail and the newcomers, eager for spoil, launched an attack upon the Indian camp some two weeks after their arrival.

It was not hard for our company, armed with new musketry and in the climate of friendship then prevailing, to fall upon the camp in the dawn while they were sleeping, and so to surprise and overcome them.

David Del Monté

I stayed with Indy at my camp, as I would not go there with arms. Early next morning, after the raid, I saw the company returning. Some were wounded, but their faces were radiant, and, with arms raised in triumph, they were singing 'Onward Christian Soldiers,' led by the pastor, wearing a silver breastplate over his vestments a dagger at his belt and holding aloft a sword. When he drew nearer, I saw that his sword blade was still wet with blood.

My boy Stephens, now five years old, could speak no English and was sullen and angry. He did not know me as his father. He and Indy viewed each other suspiciously. The men feasted and drank but that evening it became clear that all was not well. They had subdued the camp in a surprise raid but not overcome it completely. Still, we saw the smoke rise upon the horizon and as the winter drew near we could no longer go to the Indians for milk or food and we suffered. My boy Stephen, as I saw, knew me not, and he would not remain in one place. When placed for prayers, he would squirm under the pews. He went his own way; he was untameable. He only replied to our commands in Indian, and one day when most were out in the fields, he escaped.

There was anger that night when it was discovered he had gone. The reason for the raid was gone, and although the pastor upbraided us and asked us why we were not ready for another attack, the heart had gone out of our existence. The snows came. Our morale fell with the weather. Indy delighted all except the pastor who, in sermons, preached that our ills came from the stranger in our midst, the heathen that was despoiling our souls. I do not know how many believed him, but as food grew short I saw a reluctance to share with Indy among those who had shared well enough before.

Indy survived. Indeed, as our company wasted and died, Indy prospered. Where he derived nourishment, I do not know. The winter of 1611 was the worst, and it could have been the best. Ignored by the Indians now, deprived of help, we had to rely upon our own resources. Only fifty-four made it through the spring, and, weak as we were, we could hardly find the strength to plough or grow crops for the next year. We had to go to the Indians for help and the company begged me to take Indy along and see them.

And so I did. I took Indy and went to the Indian camp. They received me mutely. Without protest, without complaint, I was fed and watered there as was Indy. In the night I attended a council in which the peace pipe was smoked. I saw my boy Stephens there. He looked more grown up, if wilder, than before. I tried to speak in the Indian tongue, a little of which I had picked up from Indy and was made to understand that it was time for me to choose to stay with my own people or live with them. If I chose the latter, then I knew what I had to do.

I nodded and with Indy, returned, bearing parcels of food, which were set down before the company. While they were so occupied I stood up and said, 'They want Abrahams.'

There was silence while they stopped eating and listened.

'They want Abrahams or they will destroy us.'

They resumed eating uneasily. The Indians came upon us in the night and slaughtered our watch keeper, took our guns and our swords, and murdered all, including my second wife. They spared no one except myself and Indy.

I live now in the Indian camp and lead a good life. But of our Virginia colony there is now no trace, and I am sorry for that. For if it had not been for Abrahams there is every reason to suppose that amity would have prevailed between our peoples. My son Stephen is a fine brave now and if Indy does not have his figure, he is a cheerful fellow who can give a good account of himself.

I lay down my pen now. I have told my story. I am calm in my heart for I have done no wrong. Should anyone who comes after me read this, I ask only this: Think sometimes upon us that tried to forage in the New World that first decade of our Lord in the seventeenth century.

My boys are devoid of any desire to learn of God or our Lord Jesus Christ. Sometimes in the Indian tongue I tell stories around the campfire from Genesis, Moses, and suchlike as I can recall. They listen intently. But what the Indians love best are stories of battles, and to them, God and Satan are as tangible as I and my sons.

Sometimes I visit the camp with Indy and place flowers on the graves of my wives. I am familiar with my son Stephen because we live cheek by jowl. But yet he is more strange to me than Indy,

There. It is done now. My son will be married soon. If this parchment does not survive, there shall be no record of our brief time here. I shall be expunged, and my issue shall be of the Indians till new settlers come to wage war with my generations.

SELLING UP

Mr Huggle decided to sell up after living all his life in the delightful country town of Hibcaster (pronounced Hib'ster). He told his friendly neighbours two doors away, the Smithsons, newcomers of twenty-five years' standing, that 'yobs' were the reason for his departure. Like any part of England, Hibcaster attracted its share of the work-shy (new-age travellers), but even the indigenous population had become addicted, according to Mr Huggle, to laddish and ladette behaviour and boorish late-night drinking. Huggle would also point to indirect experiences which he summarised as 'soaring crime rate,' 'mass immigration,' 'country ruined,' 'metrification,' and a host of other ills which made Mr Huggle feel he was being trapped in the monstrous tentacles of modernity. Of course, there was more to it than that. There was the weather. Why, Mr Huggle told the Smithsons, did he have to suffer the English climate when he could retire to his house in Spain?

'But 800,000 English people live in Spain,' said Mr Smithson, 'especially round the coast. It will be like living in England, but instead of Hibcaster it will seem like Essex. They don't even speak Spanish.'

'Ah,' replied Mr Huggle, 'but I'm learning Spanish.'

What, thought Mr Smithson, to say *pan por favor* and *una cerveza*? But of course, he was too polite to tell Mr Huggle this. And after he left, Smithson washed up his coffee mug and wondered why he himself didn't go to Spain or somewhere – or anywhere – or why indeed the entire population didn't sell up and decamp to other parts of the world. He considered what Huggle had said. Yes, times were different. There were a lot of drugs around. Hooliganism and vandalism were commonplace. Perhaps Huggle did not realise that Spain was hardly the rural backwater of yesteryear when wine was nine pesetas a bottle. It was a thoroughly modern, drug-strewn place where young people did not marry and have children but went on drinking binges at the weekend just like their English counterparts. But round the coast, on the fringes, literally, of society, lived these permanently sun-tanned septuagenarians, wrinkled, nursing their gin and tonics, playing bridge, and bored out of their minds. The sun, when it shines every day, ceases to be a novelty. You curse the sweat and the mosquitoes and begin to long for – what? The vagaries of the English climate? The chance to moan? The sheer struggle of living in a crowded country?

Perhaps not. Mr Huggle returned home, which was simply a matter of walking a few paces along the pavement, and thought: 'They're just jealous, that's all. They'd all like to do it. The entire country.' He smiled to himself as he too imagined the entire British population deciding one day to pack up and inflict themselves on other inhabitants around the world. Let them laugh! The British have been stock figures of fun for years. The neat socks, sandals, and boxer shorts; the man with the binoculars aimed at the ships out to sea and more particularly, the buttocks of young girls, nymphs frolicking at the sea shore, the absurd drunkenness, the people who man the class divide, from the disgusting 'Essex man' with his pot belly and his addiction to 'English' manufactured food to the stiff accountant with his regular habits and ordered life – both as bad as each other. Supposing all these decamped? Who would want them?

But luckily Huggle was single and alone, a bachelor at fifty-three, with money in the bank and a house to sell. What Huggle did not let on was the real reason he was selling up. He could only half admit this to himself, and he wasn't going to tell anyone else.

What prompted Huggle's decision to leave the city of his birth occurred at work. Huggle worked as a cabinet maker. He was skilled and fast. But six months ago he had taken on an apprentice under a government scheme, and it soon became apparent that the boy was faster and more accurate than Huggle had ever been even in his heyday.

The boy, called Sammy, had no qualifications. He had what was called Asperger syndrome, and it was difficult to get more than two words out of him. Uncoordinated in every other way, lanky and gangling, prone to knocking coffee mugs from the edges of laminated sheets on which they perched, Sam was uncannily focused when it came to planning, lathing, sawing, or nailing. He was so fast that Huggle found himself standing around smoking or drinking a coffee when ordinarily he would have been hard at work. Moreover, Sammy was not a typical youngster. He lived with his family contentedly, had no girlfriend, and when he was not in the workshop he spent time on his computer. No one could say he wasn't a good boy, even if he was an eerily quiet workmate.

Since Huggle never liked to take on too much work, it wasn't long before Sammy was doing most of it. Huggle still accompanied him when it came to fitting, but even these Sammy could accomplish on his own without too much difficulty. The day came when Huggle returned home and found he wasn't hungry. Strange, he thought, as he sat down in an armchair and turned on the evening news. He hadn't done anything all day. He had handed a couple of pieces of wood to Sammy, who had worked like a dog, but apart from that he had stood around, smoked, drank coffee, and read the paper. He had taken a couple of calls from customers, had driven Sammy to a job, and dropped him off.

David Del Monté

The morning came when Huggle did not go into work at all. He called in and spoke to Sammy on the phone who did not reply when Huggle told him he wasn't coming in.

'Don't nod, Sammy,' he said. 'I can't see you if you nod. Are you nodding?'

No reply.

'Can you manage OK?'

'Yes.'

So Huggle stayed in bed. He went in at midday and found everything shipshape. Sammy had not only produced a beautiful cabinet; he had already put everything in order and tidied up. The place had never looked as good, not even when Huggle had first started up.

'Well done!' he said.

Sammy smiled shyly, fidgeted, and coiled and uncoiled his fingers in front of him.

'Carry on like this. You won't need me at all,' he said.

Sammy looked expressionless.

Huggle made his decision a month later and went in to tell Sammy he was leaving. Sammy could have the workshop. All he'd need to do was pay Huggle a monthly rent. Sammy, as usual, said nothing, and Huggle went off to put his house on the market.

The next morning (Huggle remembered the time well; it was 8 a.m.) he was eating a toast when the phone rang. It was the police. There had been a break-in at the workshop; could he kindly come down and see? Of course, he could. The sight that greeted him was ghastly. The workshop was wrecked. Machines had been torn from their plinths and smashed on the ground. Tool boxes overturned and equipment strewn around. It was as if a bomb had gone off.

'Can you see if anything has been taken?' asked the officer.

'Everything's destroyed!' said Huggle. 'Sammy will be furious. This was all going to be his.'

'Sammy?' asked the officer, suddenly interested.

They collected the boy from his home, a council house not far away, and brought him down.

Right away, Huggle knew something was wrong. The boy was positively shifty.

'Sammy,' said Huggle going up to him, 'do you know anything about this?'

But Sammy shifted and said nothing.

'Why?' Huggle asked. 'Why did you do it?'

Sammy now focused on him and the effect was electric. With a mouth working like a fish, his face grey, Sammy exploded, 'Because you said you were leaving. And I did everything for you!'

This was enough in the police's view to have him arrested. They took him away in a police van and charged him with criminal damage. Huggle went into the workshop and tried to tidy up. It took the best part of a week to put everything back. Apart from the lathe there was not much actual damage. It looked worse than it was.

When the court case came up, Huggle went to speak as a character witness in his defence. Sammy got off with a community service order, and after he had done his week's litter collection, he turned up at his workshop.

'Now do you want to start work?' Huggle asked.

Sammy nodded.

'I'll be going on holiday,' Huggle told him an hour later, 'to Spain. I wonder if you'd like to come.'

Sammy, about to hit something with a hammer, left it poised in midair for a second before bringing the head hard down on a nail. An almost imperceptible nod of the head gave Huggle his answer.

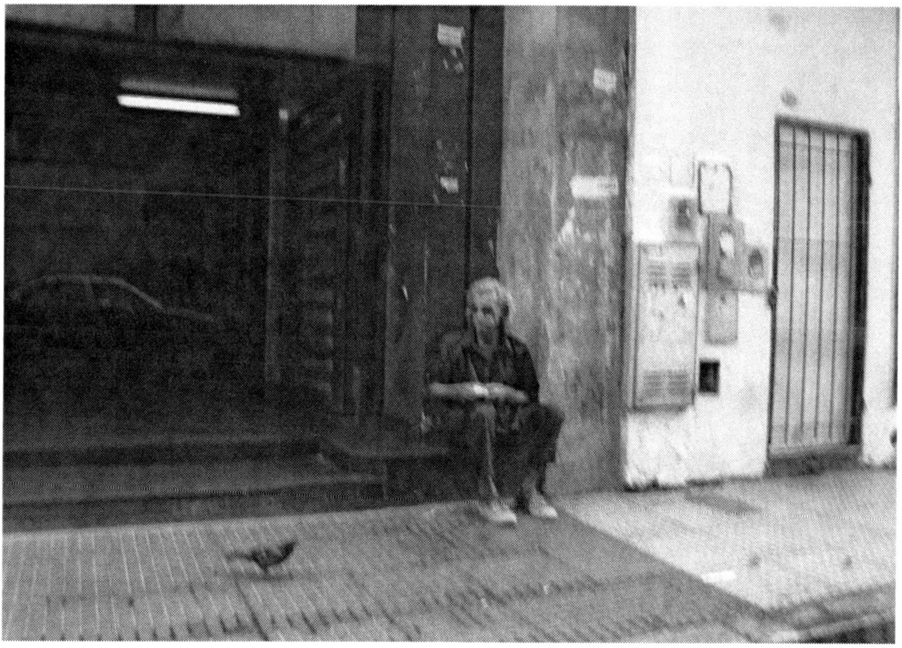

GYM MASTERS

I got to know Ken and Doug fairly well over a period of three years. They frequented the gym in the basement of the building where I worked. Despite a gap of a couple of years when I encountered business difficulties after I had re-established myself in the same office complex, I was pleased to see them again, strolling along together, hold-alls in hand, looking as trim and sturdy as always.

It was quite natural for me to stop and chat with them, and they told me they were happy to see me back. I gave them a swift resumé of my fall and rise, before recalling old times, and in particular the vastly overweight girl they used to hang around with, who always wore a red trouser suit. They told me Angie was totally unrecognisable and with a chuckle they advised that I look her up on the second floor.

I wasted no time so doing and they were right to anticipate my delight when I discovered that Angie had evolved from a gauche, immature, and frankly unattractive individual into a poised, charming businesswoman with a body to die for. Gone were her swollen cheeks, which pushed the eyes back into her head, the greasy fair hair shoved back under a cap, and the thighs bursting from their trousers, themselves of a towelly and rather unpleasant texture.

'My goodness,' I said, when I stood before her desk, staring with incredulity at the skinny young woman with carved cheekbones and beautifully made up lips and face. 'My goodness,' I repeated.

'Are you going to stand there and say that all day, Peter?' she said, angling her head in an attractively demure way, while at the same time playfully turning a pencil over in her hand.

'Well no,' I said. 'But you look so svelte, so incredible – how did it happen?'

She sighed as if reluctant to repeat an old story and told me briefly that she had been going to the gym, that was all, that Doug and Ken, as old regulars, had taken her through her paces, and that she was a new woman. She embellished this with details I frankly did not wish to know, dwelling on the changes in her sex life that had occurred.

'You certainly look like a new person,' I said.

She laughed again and I detected some bitterness.

'I was a joke!' she said. 'I was blind to the way you all patronised me! Yes you did, Peter, you can't deny it! I was too full of myself to realise that you were all laughing at me behind my back.'

'I don't think that was the case at all,' I said.

'Well, you're an arch hypocrite, the worst of the kind,' she said. 'So I wouldn't expect any other answer from you. Now, if you don't mind,' she said brightly, 'I must carry on.'

As she had not remarked upon my absence from the building (a sign, I thought, of her innate selfishness rather than dislike), I felt a few more questions were in order. She looked up from her computer keyboard.

'But you're still doing your old job,' I said.

She nodded.

'That is something I guess I'll never change,' she said.

'And, if you don't mind my saying so, when I knew you last, you were a catholic.'

'Well,' she said, 'that has changed, Peter. I'm nearly thirty. Did you want me to die an old maid?'

'Are you married?' I asked, regretting my naiveté as soon as the words had escaped my mouth.

'No, Peter, I'm not,' she said, exasperated.

She then told me of a young man, several years her junior, whom she had met on a beach in Thailand. She had been attracted to him because of his long brown ringlets (I used to have them, I told her), and they had made love within hours of meeting each other. It had been the most fantastic sex, she told me, but she knew there was nothing in it. She had her job, he his traveller's priorities. That weekend they were due to spend an orgiastic weekend together in Paris. But she knew, as he was only twenty-two, that the affair would one day be over. Nevertheless, she would have fun while it lasted.

'Why not?' I said.

Oddly enough, her sordid account acted as a bromide upon my senses, and I couldn't wait for her to complete her revolting anecdote so that I could bid farewell. Really I was amazed at the ease with which she had given herself to this man, and, I imagined, to others before him. I couldn't accept this was a recipe for happiness. Transient as pleasures were, how could they be a substitute for an enduring relationship?

I left the office wondering at the nature of her transformation. It never did to take people for granted. Who would think that rambunctious Angie, who ate and drank too much but who was known never to have a boyfriend, would turn out the way she had? The unpleasant but technically accurate slang word 'slapper' came to mind. .

The next morning as I was working out I saw Ken and Doug enter alongside each other, as they always did. While they were going through their warm-up routine, I told them I had met Angie.

'She's a fine businesswoman now,' Ken told me, stretching on the mat. 'She's making good money.'

I was annoyed at not having found this out for myself.

I said, 'She told me that you had trained her.'

'Well, that's true enough,' said Doug.

'Have you ever thought about doing that as a business?'

They looked at each other.

'I mean, you guys have stomachs like washboards. You come here every day. You could turn such experience into hard cash.'

I said nothing further about it, because at that moment Angie entered and started running energetically on the treadmill machine. She allowed Ken and Doug to kiss her on the cheeks but was somewhat cooler towards me, I don't know why.

In any case, after my session was over, a good hour before Ken and Doug's, I made my way to the management of the basement gym and asked for a franchise to run a training company there. The management took me up eagerly and so did Ken and Doug when I explained my success the next morning. All I had to do, they said, was market the project, print the brochures, and place the advertisements in the newspaper, and they would do the rest, trust them. So I did. I spent a week with designers and newspaper sales reps, and within ten days the first advertisements were appearing. I invested a considerable sum of money in promoting my gym, 'Transformations,' and immediately my industry paid off. The phone did not stop ringing with enquiries, and bookings started to roll in. The day before the first customer was due through the door, I had a visit from the local council; Health and Safety. I took him on a tour of the gym. Ken and Doug were there, clad in red and green tracksuits with the Transformations logo sewn into the breast pocket. The management had consented to the Transformations signs to be placed in suitable places on the walls, promotional items such as pens and motivational posters imported from America, and potted plants to be placed in suitable locations around the gym. It made the place look branded and professional.

'So,' the council officer said, looking at Ken and Doug, 'you are the trainers.'

They nodded, almost as one.

'And,' he said turning to me, 'I suppose you expect to restrict yourselves to adults only.'

'Come and have a cup of coffee.' I said. 'I will explain all.'

He came with me to the gym café (another innovation of mine), would accept warm water only, and took out a notebook.

'Can you give me your trainers' full names?'

I wrote them down.

'And you were going to tell me that this is an adults-only gym?'

'No,' I said, 'not at all. I intend it to be a family affair. Welcome to all.'

'Children too?' he asked.

'Absolutely. Some rich clients have indicated they want their children as young as two years old to attend, so I have designed a programme for them.'

I passed over a ledger showing my timetable.

'Do you mind if I take a copy of this?'

He scanned it into a laptop, he had already brought up on to the table.

'Well,' he said, rising, 'I think everything is in order. Only one thing, of course….'

'What is that?

'We will have to run a police check on your trainers.'

I ran and told Ken and Doug the good news including the necessity of a police check as we would be working with children.

'Children?' said Doug. 'We've never had kids here, have we, Ken?'

'No,' said Ken. 'We've never had kids here.'

'Look,' I said, 'I've invested a lot of money. I want as broad a customer base as possible.'

'Don't get shirty with us,' said Ken. 'You and your Harvard Business School mentality,' said Doug.

Of course, I knew they were only joking, so I just said, 'The police check is OK, though, isn't it, Doug?'

The two men exchanged glances, as they always did. Their charming, handsome faces were this time oddly set and expressionless. When Doug extended his arm towards me, I noticed, for the first time, a gold bracelet upon his wrist and a number of rings upon his long dark fingers.

'You've done it again, Peter, haven't you?'

'Done what?' I said, detecting, for the first time, a distinct trace of Essex dialect in Doug's speech.

'You've gone ahead of yourself,' said Ken.

'I take it you do have a difficulty with the police check.'

'Yes, Peter, you could say that,' said Doug.

I left them immediately and found my man bent over his laptop, tapping the keys furiously.

He looked up as I approached.

'All done,' he said cheerily.

'What's all done?,' I asked.

'The check. It's all come out satisfactory. He smiled revealing a set of rather rotten teeth. 'All done in a matter of seconds,' he chattered on. 'I do think you might want to study the words on your ads however. 'Experienced' and 'qualified' must mean exactly that, you know. Otherwise you might have trading standards on your backs.'

'Gotcha,' I said.

'Well,' he said, shaking my hand, 'congratulations. I admire your industry. I was going to set myself up in my own business one day, you know.' He bored me to death on how an illness of his mother had prevented this and then he'd been divorced and had been thrown off track again, all rather tedious and time-consuming .

'I admire your gung-ho attitude,' went on the gusher. 'In these difficult times, it takes real courage.'

Eventually, I managed to hustle him out and return to Doug and Ken who were both finishing a session with a client, an out-of-condition elderly lady with blue hair.

'Look,' I said, 'it's all sorted. The checks have come back negative. It's all green to go.'

'Sorted?' said Doug. 'What do you know? Did you think he's going to tell you anything here and now?'

'Look, Doug,' I said, 'I assure you he was quite happy when he left.'

'Well, I'm not happy,' he said.

'Nor am I,' said Ken. 'You should have asked us.'

'I did ask you,' I said.

I felt anger rise in me. Didn't they realise how much work I had done to set up the whole thing? Was this going to be my fate in life? I wondered.

'I can get other trainers if you wish,' I said.

'Do that, Peter. Get other trainers,' said Doug.

It wasn't as easy as all that. When I went to pay the rent, the manager told me the company did not wish to continue their association with me. He alluded, quite unfairly, to my business lapse a few years previously.

I had been holding out for a formal lease but nothing had been signed yet. It seemed that Transformations would be stillborn.

It was Angie who came to my rescue. Coming down the next morning and seeing me disconsolately taking down posters, she offered me her services in exchange for 50 per cent of the equity. This I readily gave her. What was 50 per cent of nothing?

It was Angie who sorted everything out. I don't know how she did it, but before the week was out, Ken and Doug were back on board, the management were happy, and we were really cooking. I had never been so happy in my life. My job became one of greeter and booker, while Angie took in hand the business side. With her acumen and my interpersonal skills our turnover soared. Before the year was out we were considering other locations, and Ken and Doug were being encouraged to consider making a video. Their frank and down-to-earth training approach was appreciated. People viewed the rather sadistic instructions as beneficial to their health and well-being.

It was only after eighteen months of fantastic success that I opened my newspaper in the gym café one morning to read the headlines: 'Gangland Duo in Money-Laundering Scam.'

I read with astonishment allegations on how the gym – my firm – was being used as a front for two notorious 'gangsters,' Kenneth Worsely and Douglas Chisholm, both of 21 Ninsert Road, Braintree, who had been acquitted of a number of offences due to lack of evidence

David Del Monté

or witness withdrawal. They were alleged to control an empire worth £50 million, which included, and here I was aghast, an office building in Old Street, London EC1, the site, of Transformations Gym.

I put the paper down and looked up. It was only 8.30 a.m. Doug and Ken would be arriving at 9.00 to begin the first session. They both arrived at 9.10, as bright as ever. Perhaps they had not read the story. They joined me for a coffee and asked me about the takings, as they often did.

'Good one, Pete,' they said, when I told them.

'Did you see the paper?' I asked, passing it across.

Doug read it silently, his face moving from side to side as he scanned the words.

'Good coverage,' he said. I wondered if he were illiterate.

'Is it true?' I asked.

'That is worth a lot of publicity,' Doug said, passing the paper to Ken, who read it in the same way.

'More value in those headlines than in the whole of your ad budget.'

'I hardly think any of that will attract customers here,' I said. 'Very much the reverse, I should say.'

'You're absolutely right, my son,' said Ken. 'This was Angie's idea. Set them up. Now she's going to sue them.'

'I don't get it,' I said. 'If none of this is true....'

'Who said that?' said Ken looking at me sharply. I did not like the hardness in his brown eyes and did not want to say anything more. That they were out-and-out fantasists was clear. I regretted not engaging other trainers, and of course, Angie's intervention had turned out disastrously.

'To be honest, Pete, we were getting tired of the gym in any case,' Ken said.

I confronted Angie that morning, and she admitted the whole thing.

'You won't get a penny if they can prove the whole thing was a sting,' I said.

'That's life,' she said, standing up.

And I saw for once in her striking appearance the cruelty of the young. She was amoral. They all were. I was the outsider, destined never to be their friend no matter what I did. There was nothing else for me to do but clear out. As I was sorting out my effects Angie came to me and said, with a touch of emotion, 'You're not leaving, are you, Pete?'

'Of course I am.'

She placed a slender wrist on my arm.

'I only did all this for you,' she said. 'I like you, you know. You're so stable and hard working. I was hoping….'

I shoved her arm away.

'I don't know what you were thinking,' I said. 'You never consulted me. It's over, Angie. Over.'

'Look, this wasn't my idea. Ken and Doug are media junkies… they think they're like the Krays, folk heroes.'

'Like the Krays? Are you kidding?'

I left. I was pleased to see that the gym went into liquidation that same year. The case against the newspaper never came to court. I realised that Doug and Ken hadn't really cared. They were rich after all, it appeared. Although my investigations showed their wealth stemmed more from a share in a mini-cab company than in the grandiloquent claims made for them by the newspapers. They did not have the bottle or the wherewithal to take the media to court. It was all another fantasy, and it tickled their vanity to be thought of as 'gangsters.' It was pathetic, really, that I should have bothered with such people.

I visited the council, however, to check on one thing. Did Ken and Doug have a criminal record? Was the whole affair covered up? I couldn't find out because I discovered the officer who had come to the gym had retired to Spain. He had opened up a pizzeria there, I was told, on money given to him by his aunt. A likely story, I thought. He had been bought off. That was obvious. My attempts to interest the media in this story came to nothing. I am now between jobs. I may go travelling, just for a change of scene. London bothers me now. I really don't know where I stand. I think Mexico might suit me. It's cheap there. And I understand the people are very traditional. I might meet a girl there and raise a family. As for Angie, I understand she got married recently. I admit to feeling a pang of jealousy when I heard the news. We could have been an item, if I had acted on my impulse. But I never do. Not even for love. It's too scary. Ah well, as Angie would say, 'That's life.'

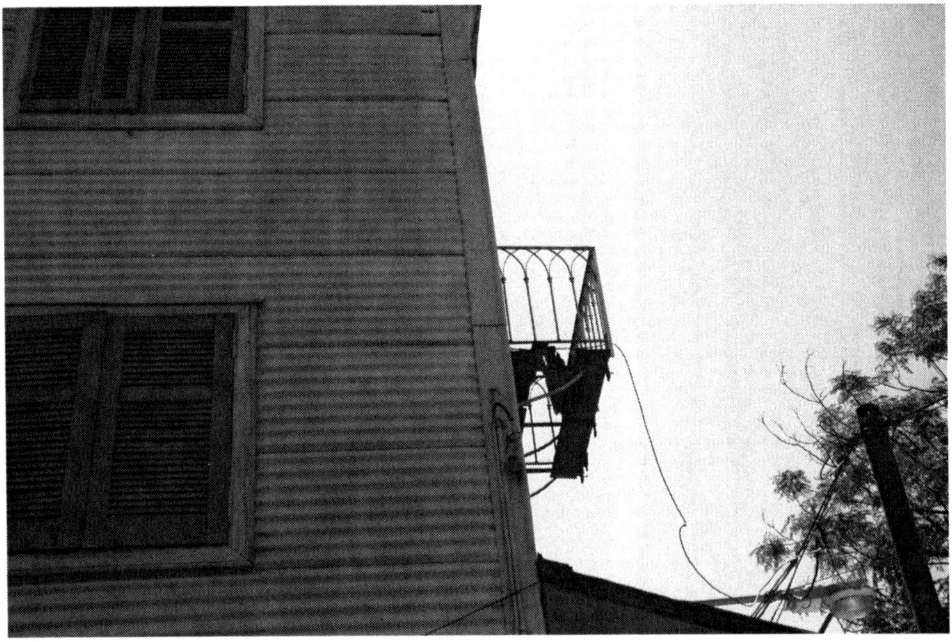

THE DEATH OF MR KAY

No one could have been more delighted than us on the day Mr Kay died, except possibly, his wife. When we heard the news, the teachers and I cut classes and repaired to the Old Tavern for a celebratory drink. That might seem callous, but Gerry, who, arguably, hated him most, reckoned that he deserved it. Sitting around that table in the bar we all resembled characters from an Agatha Christie play. None of us had killed him; he had slid away under the waves during a heatwave in Greece, the worse for wear. No, what I mean is we all had our own reasons to hate him. We all knew that as soon as he returned from holiday he would sack all of us.

He had odd irrational reasons for wanting to do this. Essentially, it amounted to paranoia. Despite all the time I spent holding his hand, he had become convinced that I was attempting to set up my own college within his organisation.

'This is really weird,' said Gerry in his Scottish accent, sipping his beer and looking rather flushed.

We all knew what he meant. The previous evening we had all gathered at the pub like men on the eve of execution, knowing that Mr Kay was due back the following day and that this would bring about the end for all of us.

'Why don't we bloody well hex him?' said Fran, my girlfriend.

'What do you mean?' Mary asked.

'You know. Put a curse on him,' she said.

Everyone laughed and carried on drinking. But I learnt that later that evening Gerry and Fran had got together, clasped hands, and prayed, yes, prayed for Mr Kay never to return.

'You're telling me that you did hex him?' I said.

'We did,' said Fran. 'And it worked!'

Our general laughter brought a Colombian student, Carlos, to our table. Looking very serious, he said to us, 'You're laughing when someone has died?'

Gerry stood up.

'He was going to sack all of us,' he said.

'But he has died,' the student said with emphasis. 'In my country we are sad when someone dies.'

'Well, for people who are sad you spend a lot of time having fiestas,' said Gerry, and we all laughed.

Carlos had been Mr Kay's cleaner. He seemed really upset, and it kind of took the gloss off our joy.

'I know he was bad,' Carlos went on, 'very bad. He say bad things. He do bad things. But he's dead.'

'So you won't have a drink then?' I said, holding up an empty glass and bursting into giggles. There was more laughter as Carlos marched off. A nanosecond passed before we regained our equilibrium.

Looking round the table I knew each of us was being glad in his or her way. There was Mary, a broad grin on her face. I remembered when Mr Kay had peered through the glass of the classroom door one morning and seen her crouching down next to a student's desk the better to see what she was doing – a not unusual act and one that was consistent with the familiarity that went on in the ELT classroom. He summoned me to the office, sat me in front of his large, partners' desk.

'Yes, Mr Kay?' I asked, respectfully.

'Sack her. Today.'

'Why, Mr Kay?'

'Because she's fat,' he said. 'I don't want fat people in my college,' he said, already reaching for a glass and a bottle.

I didn't do what he asked, but Mary had to stay away for a few days until the crisis blew over.

Oh man! The humiliation of it! The ducking and diving, the need to humour the tyrant! There was no predicting what Mr Kay might say or do. He revelled in his power. He was a one-man chaos theory, apt to upset the best-made plans. Behind it all was the use he made of the weapon he called his 'sacking stick.' Wielded frequently and without judgement it maintained a level of fear consistent with blind obedience to the whims of a madman. But he was hated for it. Myriad injustices were harboured and resentment built up.

Mr Kay was Cypriot. This was not a fact he shied away from. On the contrary he learned enough English to get by. But his mindset was, despite thirty years of residing in London, completely Eastern. The Harvard Business School might not wholly approve of his habit of humiliating employees in front of their peers, but it had been cruelly effective.

At the pub, Peter, the chemistry teacher, joined us and said he had news.

'Barry is going around crying,' he said. 'So is Doosha, and Jayboy is all but in tears.'

When we returned to the college we did find a subdued atmosphere. Despite his viciousness, Kay did have friends – those who had worked for him for a long time, and who, whether they liked him or not, were now afraid for the future. Having been successful almost by accident, Kay's riches had flowed at a time when it would have been difficult to put a foot wrong. Unfortunately, he had been on the slide for years. Those most disappointed by his death, I suspect, were his army of creditors, some of whom had been waiting over fifteen years for payment. When one of these came to my office the next day, I was amazed to discover the lengths the man had gone on his long arc towards oblivion.

Mr Kay certainly did not understand half measures. The man who wanted payment stood in front of my desk and unrolled a long till receipt, which he had stapled to a small summary. He was a Greek with thinning hair pasted over his scalp.

'Twenty thousand pounds, fourteen pence!' the man declaimed in a sing-song voice.

'Mr Kay is dead,' I said.

The man looked at me as if I were stupid.

'I'm knowing this,' he said. 'Now *you* pay. You were in our club once.'

It all fitted together in my mind. Unpleasant memories of being hounded into drunkenness by Mr Kay. 'You're from the Exclusivia Club?' I said.

'The Exclusivia? Yes,' he said, his Greek accent becoming more pronounced.

'Don't you know,' I said, 'that when a man dies, his debts die with him?'

Reluctantly, and only after more persuasion, the man departed, to be followed by several others who all vainly imagined Mr Kay would only be too pleased to jump from his grave and repay for all the nights of debauchery he had enjoyed at their expense. The only people who ever saw the colour of Mr Kay's money were the taxi drivers of London all of whom knew his home address by heart. They would return him, insensible, in the early hours, deposit him at his front door, ring the bell, and depart, counting the notes they had lifted from his wallet.

About a week after our drink in the pub, Mr Kay's two sons arrived from France where they had been living – far from Mr Kay's reach – and it was announced that his will would be read out in his main office. His wife, a mousy put-upon thing who had suffered from years of verbal and physical abuse, sat to one side. Mr Garambos, Mr Kay's lawyer, took centre stage.

The will left almost everything – which was mostly debts – to his wife. The college he left to me, with the exception of a few departments, which he left to his two sons. This was the reason he had stipulated that the will be read out. My astonishment only lasted a few minutes before I realised Mr Kay had wanted one last joke at my expense. He had left the college to me, on certain conditions. The first was that I give free education to anyone who could claim Greek or Cypriot origin. The second was that any female student was entitled to a full remission of fees. Under such terms, and with Jay there to enforce them, inheriting the school was out of the question.

'Do you accept the terms?' Garambos asked.

'Of course not,' I said.

'Very well. In that case, the college passes to Mike and Bob.'

Mike and Bob just looked steadily at me.

They had never visited the college, not once. It had always been me who had sat with Mr Kay into the night drinking, who had listened to his drivel, and who had taken him home or to a club or had seen him off on his overseas marketing trip, a cover for spending time in a local brothel.

At the end of the will reading a memorial service was announced for the coming Monday. As if nothing was amiss I was asked if I would lead it.

'It is what Mr Kay would have wanted,' said Mike, looking at me down a long face eerily reminiscent of Mr Kay's. He took me covertly to one side. 'You were like a son to him.'

My Kay's sons took over the management of the college, but they soon delegated most functions to me and one of them returned to France.

I told Mike, the remaining son, that I would assist him, but without an incentive or security I would not put all my energies into promoting the college.

'Let me be straight with you,' said Mike looking at me with his long dark face in the way redolent of his father. 'The business is bankrupt. If you want to take it over, you can. I'll just retain some of the computer and science faculties.'

I leapt at the chance, and before the week was out, I found myself effectively Mr Kay's successor.

On the day of the memorial service, Gerry asked me if I intended to say something to mutilate his memory.

'I've got his college. Isn't that enough?' I said.

'Don't you want vengeance?' he asked.

I sent him off and sat down. I remembered the first time I was sacked. I had only been there a few days and did not know how things were. It happened long after everyone had gone home. He had started drinking, and as the alcohol turned in him, he switched from Mr Nice to Mr Nasty. Snarling, he demanded the keys to the building. Having given them up, there was no one to open up the next morning until Jay arrived.

'What's happened?' he asked, passing the lines of students waiting on the stairs.

'I've been fired,' I said.

'What are you doing here then?'

'I don't know. I've come to teach, I suppose. 'He raised his hand.

'Don't worry. Just come in, carry on as normal, and when he comes in at eleven o'clock, I guarantee he'll greet you as if nothing had happened.'

Jay was right. Mr Kay made his entrance and before unscrewing a bottle of whisky, waved at me as I passed by his office to do some photocopying.

'Morning!'

I glanced in. He was all sunny smiles, hand raised. I raised mine.

'Morning, Mr Kay.'

While he was out for lunch I retrieved my keys from his desk where I had seen him secrete them the night before. Two or three nights later when the alcohol turned his mind again and the voice dropped and the order was barked at my head: 'You're sacked!' and slower now, threatening, 'Give me the keys!,' I was ready for him. I had found some old useless keys in my bedsit, and it was these I handed to him.

'Eric?'

I awoke from my stupor. It was Mike.

'You look very smart,' he said, looking at my new suit, shirt and tie. I had shaved too.

'Thanks.'

He took a seat opposite me.

'I've found a few bunches of keys in my father's desk drawer. We cannot unlock anything,' he said showing me the bunches I knew only too well, in the palm of his large, meaty hand.

'I've no idea, Mike, sorry. I can't help you.'

I just smiled and shrugged.

At the memorial service I told the audience, 'I want us to remember Mr Kay as he really was,' and I waved to Gerry on the balcony who was manning the machine to begin. When the tape began to play, it was clear something was wrong. The sound quality was very good – almost life-like, in fact – and people looked around unsure from where the sound emanated.

We heard the sound of Mr Kay pouring his first whisky of the day.

'Fuckin' hell.'

There was a ripple of laughter, and I could imagine Mr Kay spilling some over the side of his desk. I could see him raising the tumbler of amber liquid to his lips with a swift flick of the wrist. He'd be sitting, slumped at his desk, his long pasty face framed by dyed dark brown hair which was going ginger at the temples (blotches of dye had penetrated to the skin below the thinning hair.). Mr Kay had a long nose and a chin which curled up slightly, like a witch's.

He was sitting there, his potbelly pressing against the drawer of his partner's desk. He was, for him, contemplative, and sat for a few minutes without moving. Then he lifted his head and we heard him yell, 'Doosha!'

His secretary, a short, dumpy Asian girl, with a fixed smile upon her lips, entered.

'Yes, Mr Kay?'

'My letters! What are you standing there for?'

We heard her return, somewhat warily, with the morning's mail.

I could see it all in my mind's eye. And I thought, so could the audience. The girl sought to get no closer to Mr Kay's large reproduction partner's desk than was necessary to deposit her sheaf of mail and flee. She placed the envelopes upon the desk, but before she could make her escape, Mr Kay barked, 'Doosha! When are you getting married?'

She emitted a girlish giggle, which was as affected as her smile.

'Oh Mr Kay, I haven't even got a boyfriend.'

Mr Kay grunted.

'Is Barry in yet?'

'Barry's wife died yesterday, Mr Kay.'

'She did?' he grunted. 'And Abu?'

'In his office.'

'Eric?'

'Everyone's in, Mr Kay.'

There was a swish of skirt as the girl turned to go once more.

'Big Jim?'

'Big Jim?' she said, turning round to meet his gaze.

'Yes, Big Jim? Are you deaf?'

She shook her head, a little pale.

'Big Jim's in Spain.'

'Fuckin' hell! Get your uncle in here, Jay.'

He would be watching her departing rear end with, I recalled, lascivious satisfaction, licking his lower lip as he did so.

'Here I am, Mr Kay.'

At the doorway stood a smartly, nattily dressed Asian man. Mr Kay's general factotum, and the girl used his appearance to make good her escape.

'Jay, boy!'

'Yes, Mr Kay.'

He stepped up obediently to the table. He found himself looking down upon Mr Kay's leather slip-on shoes. He noticed they were rather down-at-heel. His, Jay's shoes were as natty and bespoke as his tight fitting trousers and jacket.

'Jay, boy!'

'Yes, Mr Kay?' said Jay patiently.

'What are we going to do about the English school?'

'Eric's upstairs, Mr Kay.'

'And Abu!

Can't understand what he says! Why did you hire a fuckin' Yaruba? Member of the Institute of the Management of Crap Artists, with a Master of Buggery after his name.'

The congregation laughed at this, and even the priest smiled. 'Now, Jay,' went on the disembodied voice, 'go and get Eric down.'

'Yes, Mr Kay.'

A few moments passed. The tape activated again when I started speaking.

'Yes, Mr Kay?' I heard myself say.

'Look, I want to talk to you. Haven't had a chance, have I? And have a drink. Do you expect me to drink by myself?'

'I've got to go home.'

'Go home? What home? What home have you got to go to? Just a stinking bedsit. Admit it, you've got nothing....'

'I....'

'You are nothing! Go down and get me some drink.'

'What kind of drink?'

'Brandy or whisky. And some beer. Take it out of there.'

We heard notes and a few coins being scooped up. Then his voice started again.

'I've fucked 'em all. Indonesian pussy. Japanese pussy. Black pussy. What pussy have you fucked, eh? Eric? Well, do you like fuckin'? Do you?'

The audience was sitting there, numb, frozen. His wife's face was blank; his sons were red with outrage. I had to do something.

'I like fucking, Mr Kay.'

'Of course you do. You're young. I know what you're trying to do.'

'You do, Mr Kay?'

'I'm not stupid. You sit there with your smile. I should have known. Never trust a man with a beard. And stop grinning.'

'Sure, Mr Kay.'

'Have a drink.' Here the sound of alcohol being poured into a glass. 'You're my only friend; do you know that, Eric? My wife hates me. My sons never call me. The others can't wait to get out of my sight. Think I don't see that? Now you're doing to me what I did to the school where I first worked. Introduce a few of my own students into the class, eh? Isn't that what you're doing? Offer to rent a few rooms, eh? Before long the school is yours. Isn't that what you're doing? Tell me the truth.'

'Of course not, Mr Kay.'

'Of course not! Of course not! Here, have a drink.'

'I've had enough.'

'Have a drink, damn you.' The sound of liquid being poured into glass. 'Ah, Eric, Eric, where will it all lead you, eh, this ambition of yours?'

'I don't know, Mr Kay.'

'Cheers, Eric.'

'Cheers, Mr Kay.'

At last there was silence.

'Well,' I began,. 'that was Mr Kay. We shall never forget him. He loved us all, in his way. We shall miss him.'

I climbed down and left the church. I had to go outside for some fresh air. I felt Mr Kay in my head, buzzing. In the days and months that went by, I felt Mr Kay was watching me. As I sat at his desk and made my decisions I found myself thinking what he would say and do in those situations. Sometimes I found myself even sounding like him.

But of course, I could never end up like him. Not in a million years.

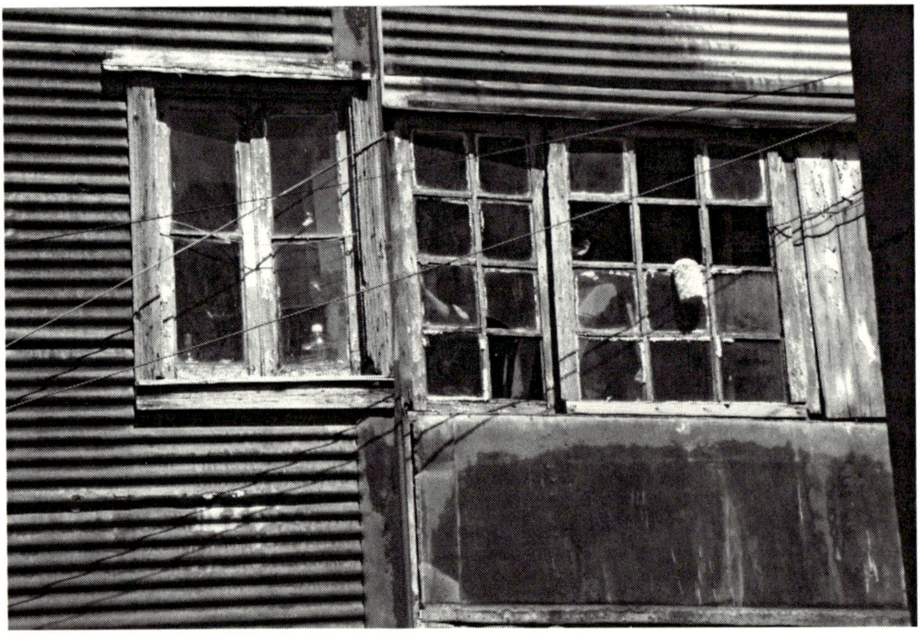

GHOST STORY

When I worked for His Lordship, I was not intending to betray him. He gave me complete liberty to roam within his commercial premises near Bond Street. He was a canny man. The family had been, for generations. The first was a mere Mr Digby when he started out, a butcher's son from Shrewsbury. By the end of his life he was a knight; his son became a baron, and his son a duke. Each generation possessed a shrewd head for business, helping to separate aristocrats from their estates when the latter succumbed to their gambling debts. By the time His Lordship came along, the property empire was massive, a fact I can swear to having seen the shelves in the basement groaning with ancient parchments and title deeds.

Most lay thick with dust, done up with coloured ribbon, inscribed in spidery dip-pen copperplate calligraphy, hard to decipher. I was amazed how much of London His Lordship owned. His forbears had

David Del Monté

gazed upon open fields, around Buckingham Palace, Belgrave Square, Park Lane, and had built. The family never parted with a freehold.

From time to time as my duties allowed, I dipped into some of the more interesting documents. I got into the habit of noting down salient facts, such as the purchase price and tenancies, the status of buildings, and so on. It became a kind of hobby, I suppose. At the end of it I had a fair idea what His Lordship was worth.

My employer himself was a kind man. For all his money, His Lordship preferred the familiar to the new. The curtains in his office hadn't been taken down and cleaned for a generation. He preferred to wear a brace of suits with the tweed giving on the elbows than newer, flashier clothes. At sixty-two, His Lordship was married, but childless. He would come in two days per week, sit at his desk, receive calls relating mostly to his appearance at one charity dinner or another, and depart for the country. One morning I saw him stagger outside his study.

'Are you all right, sir?'

'Run across the road to the Old Cock, will you, boy, and get me a brandy!'

'I don't mind doing that, sir, but….'

'But what?'

'It's closed.'

'Get them to open up. Matter of life and death.'

He slipped into a satin-covered chair at the corner of the corridor.

I ran across thew road and yelled through the pub letterbox. I told them it was for His Lordship and they gave me an entire bottle of brandy, complete with optic. I had to turn it upside down and pinch out the 25 ml measures into a wine glass for His Lordship one after the other. Between throwing back the slugs one after the other, His Lordship stuttered: 'Couldn't believe my eyes' – gulp – 'a woman in a pink ballroom dress' – gulp – 'just appeared through the solid wall as real as you are' – gulp – 'looked at me… beautiful face, golden hair, in ringlets, dress to the ground' – gulp – 'what do you make of that, eh?'

'Where did this take place, sir?'

'Just along the corridor there.'

I left His Lordship's side and padded along the wood-panelled wall until he yelled out, 'That's it. That's where she came out!'

I tapped on the wall. It felt solid enough.

'She just came out of that wall, stared at me, and disappeared into thin air. Just like that.'

From my hours in the basement, I knew all about the building. The wall had been put up 140 years ago, and that behind it was a ballroom. The place had once been occupied by the infamous drug addict and epicure Count Vlodyvostok. I decided to tell His Lordship what I knew.

He suddenly seemed to notice me for the first time, fixing me with liquid blue eyes. Though his blond hair was turning grey at the sides, I could still see, in the long face and prominent nose, the long line of his male ancestors. 'Who are you?' he demanded, suddenly putting down his glass on a small but exquisite Regency occasional table.

'I'm Peter, sir. I went to the pub, I....'

'What do you do here?'

'I'm your cleaner.'

He stared at me for a few seconds, picking up the glass again to drain the contents.

'I see. Well, run along.'

'When your family acquired this building from Lord Darlington, who lost his fortune at cards, it was a mansion then, sir, not sub divided as it is now. Your great, great, great grandfather, sir, ordered his underlings to go by and take possession of the house. But when he did so, he discovered Lord Darlington's family was still in residence. He did not have the heart to evict them, but move they did, in the end. Your forbear kept the house empty for some months, and that was when Vlodyvostok moved in.'

'A squatter, was he?'

'That is just what he was, sir.'

'Extraordinary thing!'

'Vlodyvostok came to London with a foul reputation, sir. Yet he had riches aplenty. And your forbear could not resist the temptation to go and see if he could divest him of some of it. Night after night they played cards, sir, each trying to outdo the other. Fortunes were staked and lost, but in most games it was not the principals themselves that fell by the wayside but lesser mortals who had not the skill or the daring to last the course. Bottles and bottles were consumed, sir, and the women floated around till dawn, bringing food and that newfangled invention, sir, the sandwich.'

'And then? And then?' His lordship's cheeks were crimson with delight, his lips wet with anticipation.

Before I could continue, one of His Lordship's suited assistants approached, giving me a cold eye, and whispered in his ear. His Lordship nodded and put on that pious expression he adopted when attending to matters of duty.

He rose, dusted his trousers, and departed. Even as his hands flecked the dust from his clothes I could see the be-ringed fingers of his forbear, the satin pantaloons and crisp white stockings, the fancy shoes and the calculating sloping shoulders. I went straight to the library and read up everything I could on the family. I wanted to be sure that when the ghost came again, I would be ready.

Unfortunately I was dismissed a week later, and the ghost did not reappear. I hung around jobless outside the premises for a few days, until I caught His Lordship coming out. He was making for his car, the chauffeur holding the door open.

'Yes?' he asked when he saw me blocking his way.

'I'm Peter, sir, remember? I got you the brandy from the pub after you saw the ghost?'

'Of course, Peter. Yes?'

'I've got the sack, sir.'

'Have you? How very unfortunate. Now, if you'll excuse me, I have an engagement.'

He tried to brush past me, and without physically hindering him I managed to blurt out some words that made him stop.

'Did you identify the lady you saw, sir?'

'The lady I saw?'

'The ghost, sir.'

He seemed momentarily unsure. It was an experience he had clearly closeted way in the back of his mind.

'I know who she is, sir.'

He paid no notice, and I watched him move off in his Daimler leaving behind a slurry of blue exhaust. Suddenly the car stopped, and then reversed. The window wound down.

'All right, I tell you what. Hop in if you've nothing better to do. And you can tell me until we get to my engagement.'

I slipped across the pungently smelling leather seats of the Daimler and sat next to His Lordship as we purred our way across London.

'No drink for me, sir. I haven't eaten,' I said, refusing the decanter His Lordship had removed from a walnut veneered cabinet attached to the back of the front seats.

'Matthew, what time is my engagement tonight?'

'Eight o'clock, sir.

'Good. Belgrave Square!'

Much as I appreciated His lordship's charity after I had eaten in the kitchen of his townhouse, I felt a fever coming on. A doctor was called, pills were prescribed, and I ended up being put to bed in a room in the attic where all the domestic staff were quartered. In the morning I felt better. I washed and dressed and came down late for breakfast. I found His Lordship reading *The Times* in the morning room. He looked up as I entered.

'Yes?'

'I just wanted to say thank you, sir.'

'Well, do you know the identity of that lady that I saw?'

'She was the wife of your great, great, great grandfather, sir. Seduced by Vlodyvostok and kept in the house you owned until she died, sir.'

'How did it happen? Tell me, boy.'

'One night, Vlodyvostok and your ancestor were playing cards in the ballroom near the great roaring log fire. It was winter, sir, and

David Del Monté

snow lay all around. Vlodvokstok always had a small band playing gypsy songs, and a gaggle of women to entertain the nobles between games. The stakes were high. It was all or bust. Your ancestor had lost everything. The 40,000 acres in Ireland, the townhouse, the country pile in Durham. All had gone to Vlodyvostok, the blood-eyed demon from Bohemia. Then the count made his diabolical suggestion: 'Give me your wife and you can keep your fortune.'

'And what did my ancestor do?'

'What your ancestor dreamt up was a plan so ingenious, sir, that only an agile brain could have conceived it. The next evening was deemed the time of exchange. Your ancestor came not with his wife, sir but a rapier. There was a fight, and Vlodyvostok was run through the gizzard, the point entering and exiting from his back. The count warbled blood, threw his head back, and laughed. Taking out his own sword he chased your ancestor round the room, before collapsing. Your ancestor took his wife and left, leaving the count for dead. Late that night he received a message delivered by his odious servant, the noxious Biddulph: 'Deliver up your wife, or take the consequences.' Of course your ancestor refused. But a bargain was a bargain. Willingly or not, he had to give her up. But he sent his lady's maid servant instead, who looked very like his wife. This ruse did not deceive the rapacious count.'

At this point we were joined by His Lordship's wife.

'Just been hearing about the ghost, my dear.'

'Indeed?' she enquired.

'Young boy here says my ancestor sold *his* wife to settle a gambling debt. Don't think I'd do that to you, eh?'

'I expect you would if you had to. They say ice water runs in your family's veins, not blue blood.'

His Lordship rose and shook my hand.

'Well, my boy, I thank you. Most entertaining. Come by my office later on and I'll have something for you.'

I was glad to comply. First I took a detour to my Brixton house to change my clothes. My friends there, all actors, were curious as to my experience of the previous evening, but I didn't have time to tell them much. I hurried to Bond street to pick up what I hoped would be a decent reward for my researches. But when I arrived, I was told he wasn't there. I thought the receptionist on the ground floor was being obstructive.

'Look,' I said, 'I know I was sacked. But you don't have to lie. His Lordship asked me to come by.'

The girl's wide-eyed protestation told me I was way off the mark.

'It's not that,' she said. 'It's just that he's disappeared.'

'What do you mean?'

'He was here this morning, but he just vanished. Security is looking all over for him. He must be in here somewhere. We have cameras everywhere.'

It was only when security descended to the basement that they picked up the most egregious smell. Something down there was rotting. Following the odour they came to a small bare cubicle where a number of freshly slain pheasants were hanging. There too, stood His Lordship, hooking up the last of the birds from a sack at his feet.

'You're just in time!' he said, looking round and smiling. 'I wanted you to have a brace.'

We went upstairs and His Lordship went into his private office to await the arrival of his wife, who had gone out shopping.

I went home. A few hours later, His Lordship's black Daimler appeared outside my house in Villa Road, Brixton. It attracted some curious glances from the drug addicts and dealers hanging around. The chauffeur asked for me to accompany him to His Lordship's home.

When I arrived, I found him in an agitated state.

'Please go in and see my wife. She's in a terrible state.'

'What happened?'

'I'll let her explain.' His Lordship's house had a grand staircase. What I liked best about it was the way it swung round grandly. I especially liked the short steps. You could easily go up or downstairs without causing a wrinkle in your gown. I paced softly upstairs on the deep crimson carpeting. Once on the landing, I quickly found Her Ladyship's room. I knocked and entered.

Her ladyship was tucked up in bed and the lights were low. I could tell she wasn't asleep.

'Who is it?'

'It's me, ma'am, Peter.'

Her Ladyship was ensconced on, or rather inside, a large four poster. I held one of the posts and stretched.

'Your husband told me you'd had a fright. Can you tell me what happened?'

'I was sitting here alone, in the drawing room, when the lights went low, for no reason at all. Then, at the window, there appeared a man dressed in black, wearing a top hat.

He stared at me. I'll never forget that face. It was so…bestial. It made a shiver go down my spine.'

I was allowed to go downstairs to the kitchen to make myself something to eat. Later His Lordship went out to an engagement. I was given a lift back to Brixton and that, I thought was that.

The next week I read a curious item in the newspaper. It appeared that while undergoing 'renovations' a coffin, about six feet long had been rediscovered at His Lordship's premises, in a hitherto hidden room. The box was finished in expensive black lacquer and its lid was

David Del Monté

missing. More peculiar was the suicide two days later of Her ladyship. She had been found dressed in a pink ball gown, in the garden at 6 a.m. by one of the gardeners. They never found what killed her. But I have no doubt it was Count Vlodyvostok, claiming his prize at last.

VALENTINE

I still remember the second time I saw Valentine, fifteen years after I had first met him. Some funny things happened back then, which really don't matter because they belong to another time. Valentine was an eccentric. His antics were subject of amusement, even more so because he was totally unaware of what a figure of fun he was. Valentine lived with his mother, was in his forties but looked younger. He carved out a meagre living as an EFL teacher. His gentleness excited aggression and derision, masked by the normal courtesies of everyday life. Well, this was the Valentine of so many years ago. And when I moved on, so did he, to another job in another school and I did not hear about him again. That is, until now.

I saw him out of the first-floor window of my bedroom, which faced the garden near the border of my beautiful bed of roses. I had opened the window and the sound of my unlatching the old-fashioned (but still perfectly serviceable) frame caused him to half turn and that is the image I have of him that stays with me still. His smooth face, wearing the quizzical pout, the pudding bowl haircut, the straight dank hair that flopped 'like a mop on a distaff,' as Shakespeare might have put it, the nylon shirt, the slacks, the slightly oversized ears, and potato-shaped nose – this was Valentine. There he was, in my garden, half turning towards me, standing with one foot on a garden fork, staring at me.

It was one thing joking about Valentine. But it was quite another to see him in my garden. I went down to find out.

'So... how are you doing?'

He gazed back at me, the weak grin still fixed upon his face. Really he looked no different to how I remembered him. He still maintained the diffident manner, recoiling ever so slightly at my words as if they were missiles aimed at the core of his being. This diffidence always aroused aggression in me, made me feel powerful as if he was a flower and I could crush him if I so wished.

'Michael?'

'Yes.'

The least I could do was extend a hand, and this I did. Keep it civilized. Why not? After some gentle questioning it transpired that Valentine had placed an advert in a local newsagent as a gardener, and my wife, not knowing who he was, had hired him. It was not a scenario I relished one bit. He still exuded creepiness, the way a rotting vegetable does. There was always something unwholesome about Valentine. The guy just wasn't male enough.

There are people who seem to be so innately unhealthy that one actually recoils from them. Their presence, even the sound of their voices combine to repel. As eager as he was to bring me up to date as to his doings over the preceding fifteen years, the less I wanted to hear.

The best I could do was exchange a few words and then, mentioning pressures of work, back off into the house, where I had occasion to question my wife as to her judgement.

'I wasn't to know he's a freak,' she said, followed quickly by, 'Is he safe around the children?'

'As far as I know.'

The easiest thing to do would be to let him go. Just have a quick word and an excuse – such as lack of money – whatever – and that would be that. So I went to the garden to tell him. I found him hoeing my small vegetable patch. In the couple of hours that he'd been there, he'd done a fair job. I felt a brute, but there was nothing else for it.

'There's been a change of plan, Val,' I said, when I rejoined him. 'We can't keep you any longer. Terribly sorry.'

His face dropped.

'Why? What have I done?'

'It's lack of money – we can't afford you.'

'Oh that doesn't matter! You see, I'll do your garden for free! My mother left me well provided for, you see!'

His face brightened, and he turned to hoe even more energetically than before.

I could find no more reasons right then and there so I retreated to the kitchen to consult. My wife and I both looked out of the widow and watched Valentine as he feverishly worked the hoe up and down the vegetable patch as if seeking redemption for some terrible act he had committed.

'His mother died apparently leaving him some money – doesn't need our wages,' I muttered to my wife.

'If you can't get rid of him, I will.'

'Don't upset him,' I said as she departed, briskly walking down the crazy paving to where Valentine stood. I remained at my post, shielded by the window. I watched her mouth shaping words and I saw his wounded face before the words came tumbling out, showering over her, deafening her, blanketing her mind with insurmountable reasons and explanations, avowals and protestations, accompanied by ever-increasing theatrical gestures, until I saw her shoulders drop and her back weaken. Keep strong, I willed to her, don't give in.... But then I saw him walk away, down the path and out of the side gate, never, I hoped, to return. My wife came into the kitchen and put on the kettle. I got up and embraced her.

'Thank you, darling. I'm sorry I was such a wuss.'

She puckered her lips and kissed me.

'That's O.K., sweetie. It's done.'

***

To say I loved my wife would be an understatement. I was crazy about her. We had our ups and downs, of course, as everyone does, but I felt safe with her. I felt affirmed and complete somehow. I loved being next to her and hearing her breathing. I enjoyed being in her proximity. We had an easy unforced intimacy. Whatever happened in my life, I felt, as long as I had her, everything would be all right.

My knowing Valentine pre-dated meeting my wife. But that night in bed I talked to her about him and made her laugh. I liked hearing her laugh. When she laughed, I knew that she loved me and that gave me a warm feeling inside. It meant that everything was going to be OK, and life was sweet, despite the temporary setbacks and difficulties that afflict us all. When she laughed and smiled, I could see that she wanted me and making love to her made me feel even better.

Three children had come out of our union, a boy and a girl, in their early teens, and an afterthought, now two years old. He was a bonny blonde-haired boy. We enjoyed bringing the family up through their various stages of development, and, until the youngest came along, were looking forward to some time being by ourselves. But Danny was a darling little boy, barrel-chested and tireless, funny and twinkle-eyed. Who could resist him?

Our marriage just was. I couldn't say it was definitively happier or unhappier than others. Memories accumulated like beads on a necklace. It was unthinkable we would ever break up. A stash of photographs bore witness to countless holidays and family events. The hairstyles and fashions changed, ludicrously so. The onset of ageing showed itself only too well. The photographs showed everyone smiling at the camera as if all the participants were happy all the time. If one believed photographs, no couple would ever split up. But the laminated images caught only a fleeting moment in time. Who saw the faces after the camera shutter had clicked?

Trust was always a big thing for us. The accumulation of the beads on the necklace had seen to that. I conformed to a recognisable set of behaviour patterns; and so did she. We inhabited a haven where we could enjoy each other. It was a warm, comforting place to be. The marriage was also an investment, a place where each of us had contributed a lifetime to bringing up the kids, our careers, and our home.

These externals – our house, our family, our careers – all became checklists by which we measured and calibrated our success and happiness. We could note them: paid off our mortgage; built the extension; private school for the eldest child. Although we did not like to admit we lived a bourgeois life, that was what it amounted to. And we liked it.

And that was how it was until, about a month after my wife had chucked Valentine out, something happened.

I had been working hard. That was always my way. I wanted a comfortable life for my family and myself. It reinforced my image of myself as a man and gave me pleasure to provide for my family and make them comfortable. Despite doing well, I always felt I could do better. I never sat back on my laurels. I always pushed myself harder and harder, and I am glad to say my industry paid off. I managed to make a few canny investments. I might even be able to take early retirement. I was still miles behind what those in the States might expect from an executive package. I knew of men as young as thirty in Seattle who had thrown in the towel, multi-millionaires. But by UK standards I worked out that I was in the top one percentile. Just as nature abhors a vacuum, a wife dislikes an expanding bank balance, and will work hard to empty it. I also spent hard, buying myself electronic goodies and a new motorcycle. My wife took up membership of a gym and devoted a lot of time to playing tennis. I could now afford to put my son through private school and of course, there were my older children's university education to fund. It all went swimmingly, but I had to work hard for it, and I did.

Sometimes that necessitated my going abroad to drum up business. I made sure I was never away for longer than ten days. Hotel rooms in strange cities can be lonely places, and I never wanted to be unfaithful to my wife. The love-making we enjoyed when I returned seemed to make my self-restraint all the more worthwhile. I would always return in a high state of sexual tension, almost just as eager as I had been when we first met. Of course, the usual familiarity always crept back after the first few days of mutual orgiastic enjoyment, and life would once more follow its accustomed groove, with the usual breakfast rituals and leaving and returning civilities being observed. The thrice-weekly cinema or theatre would proceed as usual.

And then, on one of these home-comings of mine from a foreign trip, my wife's behaviour seemed ever so slightly different. I could not put my finger upon it except to say that she appeared to act ever so slightly cooler towards me. I received the usual benediction of a kiss as I entered. My suitcase was opened and my dirty washing extracted and deposited in the laundry bin. We had supper, put Danny to bed, and then my wife settled down to watch TV.

'There's the tennis on,' she explained. 'I've been following it. You won't mind if I just see a bit, will you?'

I did mind. I was eager to get her into bed, as I always was after a long trip away. But I made no demur, and she settled down happily to watch the telly, while I picked up the paper. I read the whole thing back to front, and the tennis, I could see, was drawing to a close. It was almost ten o'clock by now.

'Do you want to watch the news?' my wife asked.

'No, I do not!' I said in a voice harsher than I had intended.

Before she could reply, a little face appeared at the door of the living room.

My little son ran towards me.

'Now, what are you doing out of bed?' I asked gently.

'I can't sleep,' he said.

A glance at my wife's face and her eyes glued to the TV convinced me that she would not be putting the mite back to bed. Well, there would be no harm my doing it, just this once. My wife didn't work, and I always felt that as I was the breadwinner, the child care should naturally delegate to my wife. But I did not hold any dogmatic views about male and female roles.

Putting my little boy to bed took some time. He hadn't brushed his teeth, I noticed, and his nappy was done up rather sloppily. So I took him to the bathroom and adjusted the nappy properly, kissed him, and stayed with him until he gradually fell asleep, eager to go downstairs once more.

When I finally crept back into the living room muttering a few gentle words of reproof about the nappy and the neglect of teeth washing, I found my wife on the sofa, her head lolled back, breathing gently, her eyes closed. The TV was still blaring away about some atrocity in the Middle East. I tried rousing her but to no avail, and I just took myself back off to bed. I got changed, underwent my usual ablutions including having a shower, and was pleased to find that my wife had woken up and was in my bed. I crept in next to her, pleased that she had laundered and changed the bed linen. She allowed me to cuddle her close but, complaining she was still tired, rolled over to go to sleep once more. I accepted this, as one must, and nuzzled close to her, coiling my body in a S shape around hers, wrapping my arm round her, and laying a proprietary hand upon her breast, as I always did. She reached up and turned off the light.

'Darling,' she said softly in the darkness, 'don't take this the wrong way, but I wonder if you could sleep in the spare room tonight?'

'In the spare room?' I said. 'Whatever for?'

'It's just that… you know… when you come back from your trips, you are usually so tired you make an awful noise with your nose.'

'My nose?'

'Yes.'

'You mean I snore?'

'Well, I don't want to hurt your feelings. That is why I haven't mentioned it before. I am sure it will be OK tomorrow. It's always just on the first day you come back.'

'Darling,' I said, 'I've spent a whole week without you. I need you.'

There was silence.

I kissed her back, then her shoulder. Gradually she warmed up. I knew she might have closed in upon herself, during my absence. What she had said was not in character. In the past she had never been anything other than eager to accept my embraces. That night she just tolerated them. Still, in the morning I felt in a wonderful mood. Like most men it does not take a lot to make me content. Success in business, a loving family – what more could anyone want?

My wife seemed happy in the morning and no more mention was made of my sleeping in the spare room or of my snoring. Everything seemed back to normal except that when I returned at the end of the day and wanted to relate my comings and goings and stuff that had happened at work, my wife seemed only to half listen. Often she watched telly, and usually it was tennis matches in some grand slam tournament somewhere on the planet.

And then… and then one day it happened.

I returned home early to find Valentine there, drinking tea with my wife. In my kitchen.

'Well, what a surprise!' I said as urbanely as I could.

She smiled at me in a friendly and wifely way but remained where she was sitting. Often she would get to her feet and pour me a cup. But not on this occasion. But I wasn't offended. I helped myself and tried to act natural. What wounded me was her smile. I had always trusted the emotion behind the facial expression. But now I hit a problem. The smile looked fake.

'What are you doing here?' I asked Val.

'Oh,' my wife cut in quickly, too quickly, I thought, 'Val wants to offer himself as a babysitter.'

I glanced from her face to his. He wore the triumphant expression of a man who knew something I didn't. He relished the rare moment of power he possessed. Sitting there, in my modern kitchen with the latest granite surface and light oaken doors, he was resting his legs up on my chrome bar stools.

'I really don't think that is necessary,' I said.

'I know what you are thinking,' my wife said. 'You don't think Val is a known quantity....'

She ignored my meaningful stares, and Val chipped in, as her ally 'I'm a known quantity all right!' he giggled, and to my horror, Susan giggled too, just like him. They must have spent time together for her to sound just like him. They must have bonded in some way; their personalities must have become merged somehow. I tried to curb these tendentious sentiments, but my mind was racing.

Val looked as if he had just swallowed the cat's cream. He was enjoying every moment of what he hoped would be my discomfiture. But I was not about to give him that pleasure.

'It's good that you guys have been keeping each other company while I've been busy away. But I need some nights in, so we won't need a babysitter just now.'

The words sounded pompous as soon as they were out of my mouth. There I was, playing the wronged husband, he the upright citizen.

'That's OK,' he said. 'I quite understand. Why don't the pair of you come round to my flat sometime. Meet my wife.'

'Your wife?'

'We live just behind your school,' he went on.

After he had departed, I asked Susan, 'If you went out, who looked after Danny?'

'Val came here.'

'I see.'

'He lives in the council block in Hodford Road, Flat 17.'

'How extraordinary that I haven't seen him around.'

'But he sees you.'

'Sees me?'

'Every morning talking to a crippled Chinese girl, who walks her mongrel terrier along the back alley outside your office.'

'He says I talk to a Chinese girl with a limp who walks outside my office?'

There was a silence. My wife put on an expression I had never seen before and would not like to see again. Her lips compressed tightly together and her eyes seemed to shrink. She did not look pretty; she looked positively scary.

'I didn't say she had a limp.'

'You said she was crippled.'

'It's not the same thing!'

Her voice was louder than I'd ever heard it before.

'Hold on a moment, darling. I may have glimpsed this girl.'

'I thought you might have done. What's she like?'

'Plain as hell. One leg is bent, from polio or some such other condition.'

'Val says you watch her gyrate up the alleyway, small dog in tow, every morning.'

'Maybe *he* watches her. *I've* got better things to do with my time!'

I was rather miffed but also impressed at the way she had turned *her* deceit into an attack upon me. Then she smiled.

'Darling, I was having you on! The woman is Val's wife. And I'm not surprised you've seen her around. She's a devout evangelist. So is he.'

I forced a smile.

'I thought you were angry with me for a moment.'

'Of course not! Come here, you big bear!'

We embraced and that, as they say, was that.

At exactly 10.30 the next morning, the Chinese woman came walking with that strange lopsided gyratory movement up the cobbled alley, followed by her small terrier dog. I watched her as she made her slow progress, fascinated by her uneven gait, her odd ducking posture. She headed slowly and purposefully towards the same block where my wife had told me she and Val resided. Her face was set tight in concentration, as it always was. I left my office telling my staff I would be back after ten minutes, and followed her. I caught up with her just as she was about to insert her key into the latch of the block of flats in Hodford Road.

'Excuse me!'

She turned and looked at me. Her face was round, not especially young or especially good-looking. She wore simple cord trousers and a jumper. A couple of small blue earrings pierced her ears. Her only sign of attention to her appearance was the fact that her black hair, cut to the shoulder, had been permed.

'Yes?' she asked, in an already very detectable Chinese accent.

'You don't know me,' I said, 'but I see you sometimes walking up that street beside my office. I work at the school. My name is Michael. I am married to Susan Wilding.'

She smiled showing all her teeth and most of her gums.

'My husband has mentioned you. Would you like to come in?'

'OK.'

I followed her into a narrow staircase and up on to an antiseptic hallway, painted institutionally with flecked emulsion. She opened a modest little front door and we entered into a little hallway and modest sitting room, in which a cheap sofa suite and coffee table were prominent.

'Would you like a cup of tea?'

I nodded and she crabbed her way into a tiny kitchen. When she came back in I said, 'Look, can you do me a favour? Can you ask your husband not to go to our house anymore?'

She laid down the tea things.

'You know I can't very well ask him to do that. If he feels there is a mission.'

'I'm sorry to hear that.'

I drank my tea quickly, although it was scalding hot.

'Don't be angry,' she said.

'I don't want my marriage breaking up,' I told her.

At this she placed her hand upon mine and smiled in what I felt was a nauseatingly patronising way.

'Trust,' she said, 'just trust.'

I took my hand away.

'If he doesn't stay away, I won't be responsible for my actions,' I said. 'I love my wife. I don't want your husband around when I am not there. Is that understood?'

'I hear you,' she conceded in the irritating Chinese accent.

Obviously I wasn't getting through.

'I haven't spent the best years of my life slaving to earn a crust for your husband to come and destroy it. I hope I am making myself clear.'

She smiled in what I expect she hoped was a beatific way.

'It is hard,' she said, 'to hear God's message.'

As if on cue, Valentine himself entered. He greeted me warmly, even going so far as to pump my arm. He was as playful as an alley cat.

'Michael here is threatened by your calling on Susan while he is away.'

He smiled at this exposure of my weakness.

'I don't want you proselytising around my house,' I told him.

'So be it!' he said, spreading his hands wide in a defensive gesture. 'But surely it is up to Susan?'

I raised a warning forefinger not too far from his face.

'Don't try it. Don't even think about it. If I hear you've been around my house while I am not there, I'll see to it that your legs are broken. You'll end up walking like your Missus.'

He just smiled when he heard this. I am not sure if he thought I was serious or whether he was so gone in his brain that the threat just did not register.

Of course he took no notice. They never do, do they? It was like a slow poison. Each time I went away, I felt Susan being suborned away from me, bit by bit. I was losing her soul, I could feel it. He was leeching it away, and I did not know how. There was nothing else to do. I went to a hardware store and bought a couple of rolls of grey duck tape. It was an easy matter to get invited in by Val's wife. Luckily I did not have to wait long. Me, with the knife at her throat, her mouth taped over, and her legs and arms tied to the chair was the first thing he saw when he entered the flat. I expected him to lunge at me with an animal roar and for me to accidentally impale him with the kitchen knife that I happened to be holding. But he did none of those things. Instead, he stared wide-eyed at me, then at her, then backed out of the flat and slammed the door. Now he was sure to call the police. There was only one thing I could do. I had to catch up with him. I left her – she could do nothing – and sprang after him. He was almost out of the front door of the building when I caught up with him. Holding on to his coat collar I dragged him back into the hallway. I looked up briefly before plunging the knife into the back of his neck. It came out quickly as out of butter. I left him there, the blood pumping out of him and ran back up the stairs, where I finished off his wife with a slash across her neck. I dropped the knife in the sink, left the taps running to wash off any prints, and dashed out of the flat and the building. Once outside, I saw that his hand was protruding out of the door preventing me from closing it. So I gently kicked it inside before bringing the door to. I then marched off quickly but calmly without drawing attention to myself. I had arrived at my car before I realised there was blood all over my trousers and shoes. Looking at the pavement whence I had come I could see traces of blood in my footprints. Fortunately the sky looked black and threatened rain. I got into the car as quickly as possible. Once in the driving seat I noticed there was blood on my face. I rubbed as much of it away with a cloth I used to clean the windscreen as I could and drove straight to a car wash. I did a pretty good job and got home with the car completely cleaned. I got into the house as quickly and quietly as I could and was banking on getting upstairs so I might change into clean trousers. Susan was on the phone when I entered, so I gazed only into the eyes of my little boy, who was standing by the stairs, uncertainly holding on to the second step. I scooped him up and made it easily to my bedroom where I tore off the trousers and put on a fresh pair. I picked up my boy and the dirty trousers and went downstairs. For good measure I changed my shirt too, and shoved them both into the washing machine, turning it to 60 degrees to get rid of any stubborn stains.

'You're a bit late, aren't you darling?' said my wife, giving me her customary kiss on the cheek. Her gesture seemed just like old times. Things were working out fine, after all. I soaked up her kiss like balm. It just blissed me out.

'Sorry, darling.' I kissed her back.

Sitting down she brought me tea.

'What do you think about having Val and his wife over?' I asked, innocently. I wanted to test the waters.

She shook her head.

'I'm through with them,' she said. 'Val is *so* persistent, you know.'

'I know,' I said.

'I just don't think I can live up to his ideals. I mean, it is possible to be good without being religious, isn't it? I think of you, darling. You're so kind and thoughtful. And you don't need religion to keep you on the straight and narrow, do you?'

'No, I don't,' I said. 'Are you saying you want to finish with him then?'

'You mean, Val? We never really got started, you know,'

'Are you sure? You can tell me, you know. I'll always love you. You know that.'

'I suppose I was a bit smitten for a while. I don't know what got into me.'

I kissed her again. She had never been so desirable. A woman is always an extra special treasure when won back from another man.

'Darling!' I said.

She kissed me back, as passionately as ever she had done before, and we clasped each other so tight we could hardly breathe. It was in the middle of this that we heard a series of thuds, the first one louder than the rest. We found him at the foot of the stairs, his neck broken. It was our little boy. He climbed stairs all right. But he never knew how to get down again. It was an accident, pure and simple. Days later the police came knocking at my door. They stayed away when they heard we had suffered a bereavement.

I dream about Valentine sometimes, especially his large hands. They are usually on my face, trying to suffocate me. I wake up and go to sleep in the spare room because I know when I dream I snore loudly. But my wife sleeps through most things now. Her pills see to that. But still we're happy. We have each other, you see. And that is the main thing.

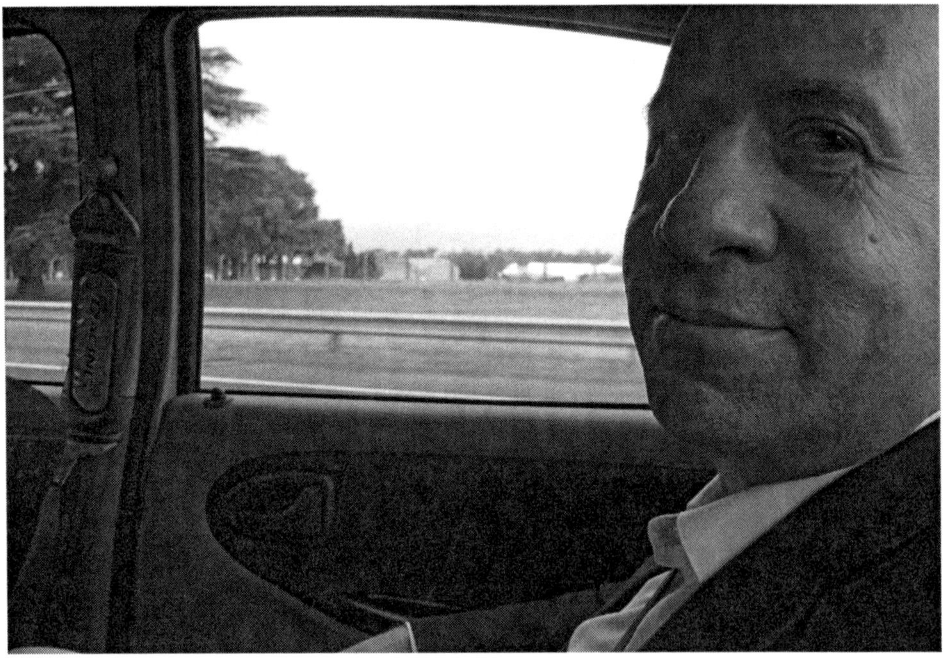

JUDE – JEW

On the day James Cohen paid his annual visit to Hotel Linden in Berlin to attend the educational agents' trade fair, something snapped. As the successful owner and manager of a small language school in London, Cohen was used to a modicum of success, and customer care was high on his list of priorities. He treated his customers the right way, and he expected to be treated likewise. Arriving one unremarkable afternoon at the hotel, to check in, Cohen was disturbed to find himself one of a scrum of guests. A group of teenagers had chosen that very moment to coincide their arrival with his. His anger rose as he observed the reception staff reacting with less than alacrity to the crowd forcing its way against the reception counter, passports in hand. But his anger exploded completely when a young male reception staffer – his crimson jacket proclaiming his provenance – announced to a dilatory black-jacketed senior: 'I'm going for lunch.'

'How dare you!' Cohen shouted.

'*Bitte?*' asked the senior.

'How dare you let him go for lunch when there are so many people to be checked in?'

The young man, with fair hair, and blood entering his cheeks tilted his chin up an inch, but it was enough to emphasise his height advantage, and he came to confront Cohen. The would-be guests made a path for him. He came and stood next to Cohen.

'Are you the owner of the hotel?'

'I might be! How do you know I'm not? I could be, couldn't I? Now are you going to check me in, or not?'

The boy – for he could not have been over twenty-five and Cohen was fifty-five – nodded in the Prussian manner, and without another word, took Cohen's passport and returned with a card for signature and a room key. Cohen departed the scrum triumphant and wandered up the lobby towards the bar area to look up old friends.

He found the bar staff winding down. It was, after all, three o'clock in the afternoon. But he managed to obtain a drink and sit quietly by himself on a small round table by the window. Within a few moments, however, he saw the bar manageress, a blonde woman in her late forties, bringing the washing out of a nearby annexe. As she walked past his window, he waved to her and she waved back in an animated fashion. Within minutes she had deposited her bag on the table next to his, accepted his offer of a drink, and was listening as he retold the story of his experience at the check-in counter. As he went over the events, blow by blow, his voice rose and he would look round furtively and repeat the story at a lower volume. He gained the impression, however, that everyone in the hotel was listening. After he had finished and exchanged trivial updates of Frau Beck's personal history about which there was nothing of note, Cohen took his leave. He picked up his suitcase and went upstairs, where he performed his usual ritual of bathing and changing before dinner.

When he came down, he sensed a changed atmosphere. He had been visiting the hotel for three years. Usually the manager himself would appear and greet him warmly, like an old friend. This time no one appeared and the reception staff, cowed by his onslaught, gazed at him like frightened animals as he strolled past. He smiled – he was generally a tolerant and pleasant guest – but met with non-committal faces. It was he turned and was already passing the corner of the reception when he heard the word '*Jude.*'

There could be no doubt about it. Uttered in the loudest of stage whispers, the word was definitely being aimed at him. It unnerved him. Not used to anti-Semitism, Cohen had no strategy for attack. Indeed, instincts told him to keep a low profile, to remain impassive at least until he had had a chance to assess his enemy.

His dinner was taken alone, in the lounge area, on a small round table. The mechanical activities of the waiter as he laid the table seemed to attract an undue prominence, or perhaps it was because Cohen was by himself that everything seemed to be that much more noticeable. Even the clack of his knife on the plate and the scrape of his fork as he scooped up the last of the gravy, seemed oddly magnified. Perhaps there was nothing in it. Eating alone is a self-conscious affair at best, and not helped by the fact that there were no other diners. He saw Frau Beck, over at the bar and waved at her. She smiled in her normal way and he smiled back. After he had finished dinner, he went over to her. She seemed very pleased with herself.

'Well?' she said brightly, when he arrived. 'Will I be getting a pay rise?'

'Do you deserve one?'

'I certainly believe so!'

She smiled broadly and served him his favourite drink: a martini on the rocks with spot of grenadine. They chatted on inconsequentially. Cohen did not mention being called Jude. What was the point? Then Frau Beck asked him when he was coming back.

'Next year,' he said, 'as usual.'

She nodded.

'You will be a big success.'

She poured him another drink.

'On the house,' she said, and smiled.

The next morning he noticed a different attitude among the reception staff. The manager, the boy who had tilted his chin at him the day before, took the trouble to come out from behind the counter to ask him if everything was all right. Well, he thought to himself, strong words sometimes have an effect!

In the evening after the trade fair had finished, he returned to the hotel to find a message. It was from a Herr Rinker, who wanted to treat him to dinner at 7.30. Nothing could have suited Cohen more. He was tired of being by himself and he hated eating alone. Rinker was in the dining room at 7.30, and he was with another smaller man whom Rinker introduced as his son. They sat down and looked at the menus. When they had ordered, Rinker said, 'I want to apologise for what happened.'

'That's all right,' said Cohen. It was not entirely unusual for Germans to apologise for the war. It was best to acknowledge the fact and pass on. What was the point of dwelling on the issue?

They ordered and the food soon came. It was more than Cohen could handle but the Rinkers, father and son, soon cleared their plates. Wine was ordered and after dinner, schnapps. Cohen soon felt light-headed and Rinker's cheeks were pink. After a pause, Rinker said, 'I will make you an offer.'

'For my business?'

'Yes.'

'I did not know you knew my business?'

'To be honest with you,' said Rinker, 'I have been the owner.'

'You have been the owner of my business?'

Rinker nodded.

'I've run it, as you can see, the best way I could. It's not been easy, especially during the cold war. But you will notice some improvements. Anyway, I've done my best. I've managed to save 30 million marks. That is my offer. What do you say?'

'You are talking about this hotel?' said Cohen.

'I know what you're thinking. Why should you sell your business to us? Why not let bygones be bygones, hmm? I wasn't the one who threw you out! That was my father. Well, not only him. He was only following orders, you understand?'

'What are you talking about?' said Cohen, suddenly alarmed.

'You are re-claiming the hotel, are you not? Isn't that what you said this morning to the staff?'

'Look,' said Cohen and he wanted to say that his wife was Chinese and that he was Jewish in name only and he was not the Cohen whose family had been thrown out. But instead he just said, 'I'll think about it.'

After the Rinkers had bowed and taken their leave, Cohen went upstairs to bed. In the morning he found his way blocked by Frau Beck. She was not smiling.

'I haf just found out,' she said. 'You are not the owner.'

'I never said I was.'

'You did! And I gave you free drinks. Now I haf to pay!'

She turned and stalked off. Suddenly, Cohen did not feel like having breakfast. He went to the reception and asked for a porter. He found he was speaking to the boy in the crimson jacket whom he had chastised publicly the day before.

'Ve don't haf any porters,' he said.

'That is not true,' said Cohen. 'Last year, as I recall, you performed that service.'

'I am not bellboy now,' the boy said. 'Herr Rinker gave me promotion.'

'Herr Rinker?'

'Ze owner of ze hotel!'

The young manager with blonde hair issued forth from the glass partition in the reception area and said, pleasantly, 'I hope you enjoyed your stay. Until next year then?'

'Next year, God willing,' said Cohen and went to fetch his case.

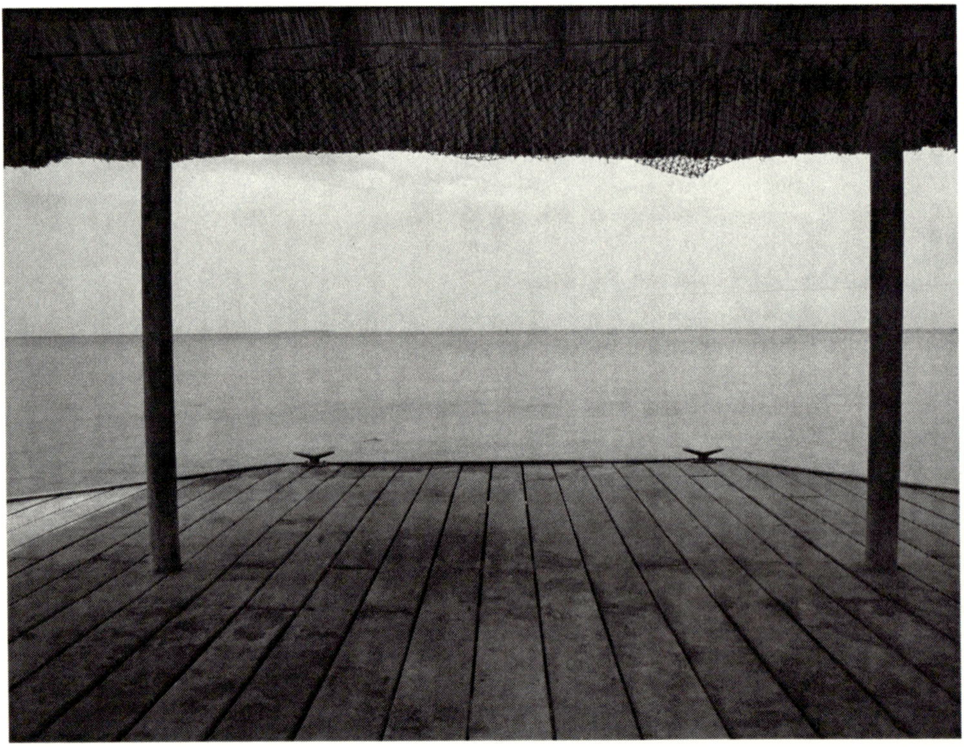

ADRIAN

On the 3 August 20--, Adrian Vincent, a five-feet six-inch, one hundred pound English teacher from Versailles, was threatened and physically jostled in the car park of the Carrefrour supermarket for no apparent reason by the much larger and heavier M. Michelle Fabian, from Paris. A week later, the two met by chance at the Place de Bastille where Adrian Vincent was taking a party of foreign students to the Louvre. There was a fight and Fabian was killed in a brief flurry of violent activity.

It was the phrase 'violent activity,' quoted by a spokesman from the gendarmerie that first drew my attention. Its cold impersonality seems to exonerate the killer. There is surprise too, that the smaller man managed to overcome his assailant. Was he armed? I read on and it appeared not. Such witnesses as there were, Adrian's party of students for instance, all confirmed that they had tried to separate the combatants and that it was only after being threatened that Adrian had struck out in self-defence.

The police had arrived on the scene in response to a call to the emergency services by one of Adrian's students. When they arrived, Fabian was already dead; his neck was broken. The investigating gendarme was much taken by Adrian's remorse.

'It wasn't my fault,' he said, 'It was him or me. But I have taken a life nonetheless.'

He was overcome with grief and the gendarme was much impressed. Adrian's tongue began to blab, and the story emerged of how Adrian had been threatened by the same man, for no apparent reason just a week before.

'I offered him everything. I said, "What do you want? Take my car, take my money." No, he wanted only a fight.'

'How did you extricate yourself the last time?'

'He just said we'd meet again and walked off.'

'We'd meet again,' parroted the gendarme and wrote the phrase down in his notebook along with the time and date.

He looked down at the motionless body of Michelle Fabian.

'He's a thug. Happens all the time. He probably has form. The unprovoked menace. The vendetta quality of his need for revenge. It all fits.' He closed his notebook with a snap. 'Don't worry,' he said. 'You could not have done anything else. This man lived by the laws of the jungle. How did you kill him?'

'I don't think I did. He lost his balance. He fell badly.'

The gendarme looked at the puny, balding figure of the English teacher, opened his notebook, and wrote reluctantly, 'fell badly.'

Even this gendarme was beginning to wonder how it was that Michelle had broken his neck by falling badly. And the exoneration? Bad memory? In the flurry of violent activity with limbs twisted, grappling, sweaty fingers clawing, fists flying; the whole puzzle prompted him to say, 'What exactly happened?'

'Do you know what it is like being small?' Adrian asked. 'I mean when you think about it, the chances of my survival in the primitive world would have depended entirely on my cunning and super-sensitive awareness, wouldn't you agree?' The gendarme nodded and only wished for Adrian to hurry up so that he could escape the scene of the crime to eat, as the delicious smell of bread from a nearby *boulangerie* was beginning to affect his concentration. 'I was helpless in the face of this unprovoked attack. But when I blow, I blow. I could either just surrender and be killed, or lash out. '

'But even so....' commented the gendarme.

'I was lucky,' said Adrian.

The gendarme took statements from the students. An ambulance came and took the body away. An open and shut case.

The gendarme, on investigation, was surprised to learn that Michelle, far from being a known low-life thug as he had imagined, was actually a professional journalist for *Canal Plus*. What was more, the dead man was engaged to be married. What on earth had prompted him to pick on a small man like Adrian?

The gendarme received several calls a week from the guilt-stricken Adrian.

'The funeral's on Friday. I don't think I should attend, do you?'

'Not a good idea,' agreed the gendarme.

'Especially as his family might be there. And my niece, Rosa.'

'Why should your niece Rosa be there?'

'She's Fabian's fiancé.'

'So you knew Fabian?'

'Not at all. I had no idea whom she was marrying.'

'Look, the case is closed. You're not going to be arrested. You're exonerated completely. All your witnesses say that you were the victim of an unprovoked attack. No one can understand it, but sometimes human behaviour is like that. Good-bye, M. Adrian.'

'Good-bye.'

Adrian did attend the funeral. Not officially of course. But he was seen at the graveyard. Everyone gave him a wide berth. No one approached him. Afterwards Adrian was heard to say how omnipotent he felt, being there. He said that everyone was afraid to go near him. It was like being Cain.

Adrian quit his job and started going to the gym every day. He soon built up quite a good physique. He said to everyone, 'I do not need to be afraid any more.'

Six months later he got a job as a P. E. teacher and asked his students to call him Mr T. They were happy to oblige.

It was a boarding school, and he was observed patrolling the perimeter fence at dusk looking, as he put it, for intruders. One day Mr T. was seen wrestling with a duck in the water and was dismissed from his job. The duck's neck had been broken. The 'T' the pupils said, stood for 'Tarzan.'

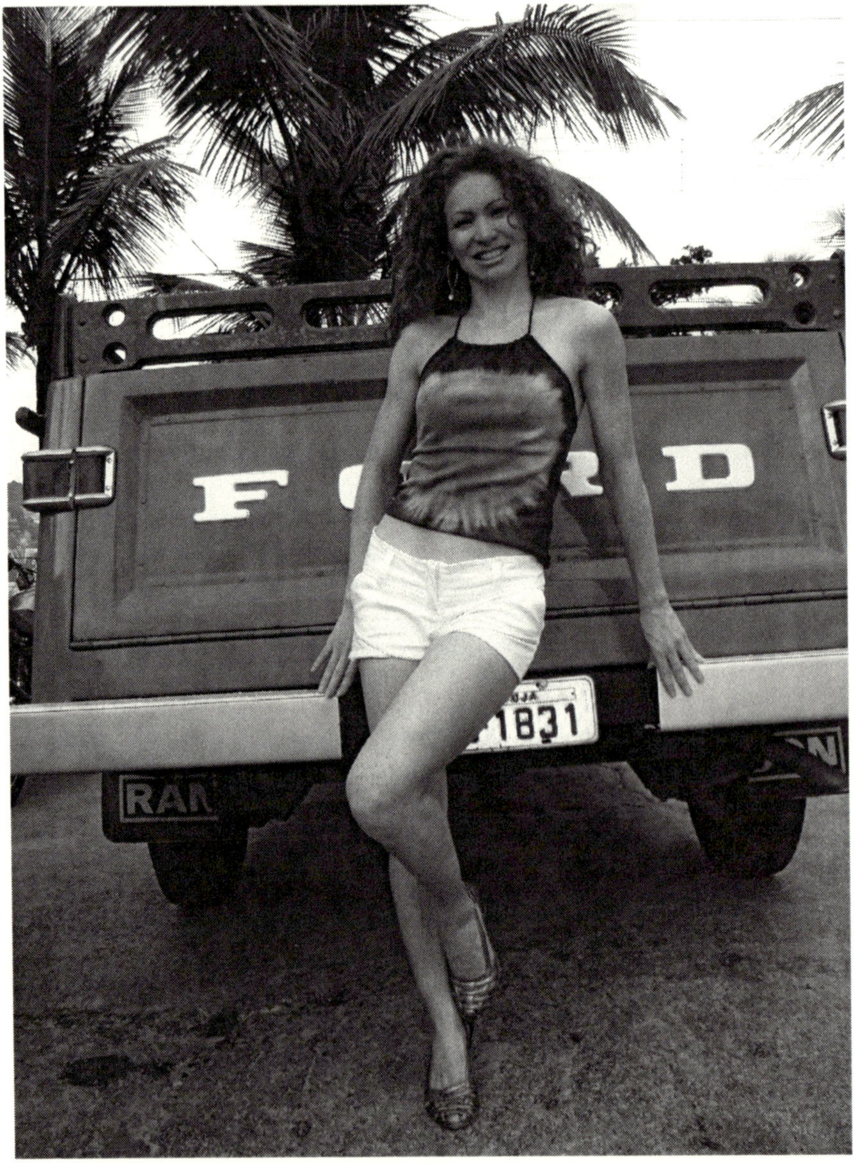
1831

WASTE NOT WANT NOT

No one could deny that the Gibsons were helpful. It was part of their liberal ethos to try and alleviate the wants of their fellow men. But the story of what happened when they took on Pete and Marilyn Jisters and their two children is a salutary lesson, perhaps, of what not to do in a crisis.

It all began when Lorelaine Gibson came across Marilyn crying in the school playground, Both their children went to the infant school and naturally Lorelaine enquired as to what the matter was. Supported by another parent, Dorota, the women repaired to a local café when Marilyn poured out her heart.

The problem was men (when was it never?). Marilyn didn't like to say it, but she was deeply envious of her two friends. Both their men went out to work regularly, brought back a thick wad, and left their wives a lot of time on their hands for tennis lessons and, well, helping Marilyn. Still, it would be rude to look a gift horse in the mouth. As Dorota balanced three steaming mugs of cappuccino from the Starbucks countertop, she dabbed her eyes, and prepared to let them in on her tragedy. It was Pete. He had lashed out at her again, taken her car keys.

'Why?' asked Dorota.

'He gets jealous. I only asked if I could go out the night before, to see me friends. He doesn't think I got a right to go out…'

The tale of domestic disharmony was ground out with several anecdotes dug up from the distant and not so distant past. They all painted, to the women, a comprehensive picture of a husband who had behaved abominably. He had treated her badly from way back. When her waters had broken, he suggested, while holding a can of Heineken, she might take a taxi to the hospital. During an argument he had bitten her nose. He often threatened to sell her car. Although Lorelaine understood that there were always two sides to every story, and that Pete must have redeeming aspects, Dorota was adamant that Marilyn must leave her husband immediately. Someone would put her and her children up for a few days, until the council found her somewhere to stay.

'But he's got a nice flat. My elder daughter….' Marilyn stated.

'How does she feel about her father?' Dorota interjected.

'She 'ates him,' said Marilyn.

'That's settled,' said Dorota. 'Lorelaine could accommodate them – just for a few days?'

Marilyn took this as a cue to snivel into her handkerchief. Lorelaine was so shocked by the suggestion, that for a few seconds she couldn't say anything at all. A vision of her double fronted period house with its Smallbone kitchen and extensive 'apartments' slotted in front of her eyes. The idyll was ruined by a thunderous roar – it was Marilyn and her brood stampeding through the house. Just as quickly the scene ended, and Lorelaine saw she was being regarded intently by her two friends. Marilyn squinted at her over her soaking hanky, far too small for the task, and Dorota, a tough, Polish women who had married an Arab and was living, as they all were, in North London. Funny, Lorelaine reflected for no reason, the families of the children in their class at school, including Lorelaine herself (she was Nigerian - her husband was Czech) were all mixed race.

'Well, Lorelaine, can you do it or not?' Dorota wanted to know.

'Oh,' Lorelaine said, snapping to, 'I'll have to call my husband.'

Truth was, she did not want to take Marilyn in – but after all they did have an annexe above the garage. Just a room, it was true, but with its own shower, toilet and a kitchenette. The family could stay there for a few days until things sorted themselves out. A quick call to her husband confirmed what she always knew – her man was generous and willing to the hilt. He would nearly always back her judgement. When he was brought to the phone, Davron did entertain some doubts, however, and freely expressed them. He did say the gesture could lead to trouble.

'Are you sure you want to meddle in other people's marriages?' he asked.

Cupping the receiver in case the other women could hear, Lorelaine replied: 'Just for a few days. Respite care.'

'All right then,' Davron replied.

So it was done. That very afternoon Marilyn drove up with her belongings stuffed in the back of her Golf; with her children, Nicola aged six, Benson, aged two. If Lorelaine had imagined the family would confine themselves to the annexe she was mistaken. Marilyn, naturally, wanted to help Lorelaine make supper (it was the cement that held the Gibson marriage together), and Nicola was upset that there was no telly in the room.

Three more people to cater to, besides her own two children, required more effort that Lorelaine had imagined. There was more to keep your eye on. Marilyn's two year old peed in one of Davron's shoes ('stop it you devil'), the two elder children had a pillow fight, and removed all the cushions from the giant settee in the living room. In the middle of this melee, Davron came back from work. He greeted the women equally, parted the children, put the cushions back on the settee, and went upstairs to have a shower.

'You're lucky with that man of yours,' was Marilyn's passing comment, and it pleased Lorelaine to hear it.

Later that evening, Davron had a long talk with Marilyn, alone, and afterwards came to bed. Then, in the early hours, there was the sound of shattering glass and a man howling in the street.

'Marileen! Mari-leen!'

There was the sound of a window opening and a woman's angry riposte:

'Get away from 'ere. This is a nice neighbourhood!'

Lights popped on up and down the street.

'I love you, Marileen! I love you!'

Locks were thrown, the door was opened, and there was a tearful embrace on the front porch of Lorelaine's double fronted house. At breakfast the next morning there was a new addition. A dark, bearded man – Pete, who, in the first light of day, and having made up with Marilyn, did not, in Lorelaine's opinion, look half as bad as he had been made out to be. But why the family wanted to join hers in the breakfast room, rather than remain in their own quarters, was quite beyond her; until she remembered, that there was no food in the annexe. Nonetheless, she strutted about getting cereal for the kids, while Davron padded in holding the newspaper (*The Independent*) as predictable as always. He seemed only mildly amused that they were a larger number than usual at the table. He shuffled about getting his own food and then went upstairs to change for work.

'Well,' said Lorelaine brightly, pouring tea for the remaining adults, 'you'll be moving back, then?'

'Er – yes,' said Pete, sheepishly. He had every right to be, thought Lorelaine.

But they did not move back. True, they loaded the Golf with belongings once more, gave hearty and well-meant farewells, made all the more heartfelt on Lorelaine's part because she was at last able to reclaim her house. And then, just as Lorelaine was stripping the sheets and putting everything in order, Marilyn and kids hove into view once more, with Pete at the wheel. She watched them clamber out and clutter her porch, standing there warily. But there was nothing to do except put on a painted smile and open the front door.

'Yes?' she said.

'Got a problem,' said Pete. He still had not washed or shaved. 'They won't let me back in.'

'What – back in your own flat?'

'Last night I had an accident. I burned it down.'

'Burned it down?'

'Chip pan fire. The firefighters won't let me back in. It's a bit wet – like.'

'That's dreadful.'

Pete and Marilyn nodded like toy dogs, and Lorelaine let them in; Nicola, Marilyn's eldest daughter was distinctly cool. She went and plumped herself in front of Lorelaine's Bang & Olufsen and wouldn't settle until *Nick Junior* had been put on. It was a SET day so the kids weren't even at school. Pete and Marliyn moved back into the annexe without demur, and Lorelaine plucked up courage to inform Davron.

'Tell them your mother's coming and you need the space,' he counselled.

But she could not do this. She could not throw them out on to the streets. In the afternoon she scrutinised *Loot* and the *Evening Standard* for places for them to live. It was a hopeless task. The flats had all gone or did not want families. And then Pete had a bright idea.

'There's a Romanian I know. He always has a few rooms. It's in Cricklewood.'

Pete couldn't remember the address exactly but he and Lorelaine agreed to go and find it. That action was forestalled by Pete finding the telephone number on a grubby piece of paper he had stuffed into his breast pocket.

Pete let Lorelaine make the call and what she heard was not encouraging.

'He left without paying their telephone bill. Do you know where they are now?'

Lorelaine looked round at Pete and Marilyn, waved and smiled.

'No,' she said into the phone.

'Don't have anything to do with 'em,' the speaker advised. 'He's always borassic. I don't know what he does with his money. Once you've got them, you're stuck with them.' And with that he rang off.

'Well?' Pete asked expectedly.

'No, I'm afraid not,' Lorelaine said.

But the Council would do something, she declared. They had to. It was the law. After a superhuman effort on Lorelaine's part, involving meetings and super-articulate phone calls, in which everything else in her life was just thrown to one side, the council did do something, despite the fact that Marilyn lost her temper at the Council man who wanted her to complete a form (which ended up torn in pieces and tossed in his face). This brought a fulsome apology from Lorelaine on Marilyn's behalf. She cited the latter's stress and promised it would not happen again. He found the family a flat to move into. The whole thing was sorted out and Marilyn did finally move out. Problem solved.

At school, during the coming week, all was smiles and waves, and even the occasional hug; until one morning when the cycle repeated itself once more. They'd had a row, Marilyn was crying, she was moving out, could Lorelaine help her?

This time, in the playground in front of Dorota and the mixed race kids, Lorelaine made a stand.

'No,' she said.

'What do you mean? No?' Marilyn wanted to know.

'I can't take you in. You've made your bed, you must lie in it. Your Pete isn't so bad. You just have to deal with it.'

'Deal with it? Its all right for you, you cow. You've got a swank house and a husband on a good screw. You've got cleaners, *au pairs*, washer women. What about me?'

The other women in the school playground watched Lorelaine beat a tactical retreat.

'You bitch!' Marilyn yelled after her, so loud that they could hear her on the street below.

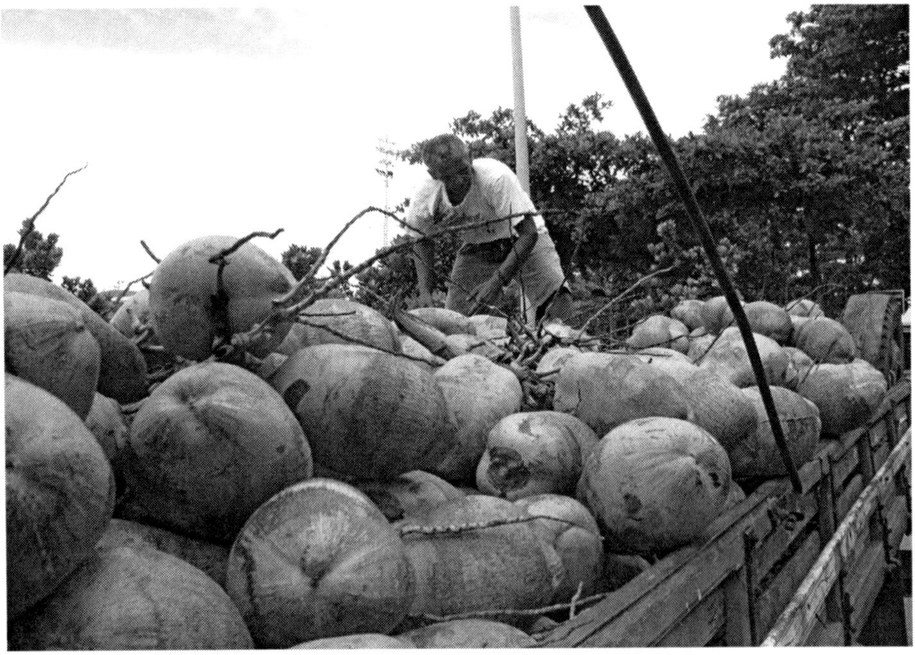

DR PLOV

When Dr Plov arrived at Tashkent airport, it was by the skin of his teeth. The Tupolov 154 M, one of many left behind by the Russians in 1990, had needed running repairs on the apron at Almaty before take-off. A mechanically sturdy piece of machinery, Plov had grunted approvingly when the captain had come on to the tannoy to tell everyone that they would not be making the journey in a Boeing 767 after all. The Tupolov, he explained, was much better in bad weather, having been built for the very conditions they were to encounter, namely driving snow and ice. The interior of the Tupolov it is true, was utilitarian, but Plov grunted again as he wedged himself between the broken tray table of the seat in front, and the wafer-thin seat. the foam of which had virtually all disappeared. The plane's roof lining was badly torn, and it had been patched rather than repaired. In other places, pieces of torn interior had just not been replaced at all. Yet, the Tupolov was a good plane. Settling down in his seat, Plov had reason to recollect the safety and security that had been provided under the old Soviet system, which the new kleptocracy had all but consigned to a distant rosy dream.

Ah, happy days!

No one had very much money but everyone was contented. Sure, everyone wanted to go to the West, but now that they were free to do it, few could afford it. Plov was different. He had been to the West many times. But he always loved returning to Tashkent. Why? The food was better, the women more docile, the taxis were plentiful because everyone who had a car was a taxi, the… his thoughts were interrupted.

'Dear Passengers!'

It was the captain again,

'Before take off, we having to make some engine adjustments. Kindly remain in your seats and refrain from smoking. Thank you! We shall be ascending very shortly. Our estimate arrival time will be affect in only marginal way. There are a ground temperature of minus ten and visibility is restrict. Thank you.'

There was a crackle and his voice was replaced by that of the stewardess.

'Dear Passengers! Thank you for fly Uzbekistan airways. We appreciate you fly with us today. We know you do not have a choice of airline when you fly to our country. In this situation you may be astonished that we bother with you at all. Dear Foreigner, we do not have much money, so money you do have will fill your suitcase full of 1000 notes if you change $200. So you may have a good time in Tashkent.'

With a start Plov realised that she had not said all of that; the thoughts in his brain had merely been spoken in her voice.

There was some muttering among the staff in Russian and Uzbek before someone realised they had read part of the announcement given out at the end of the journey.

The tannoy came on again.

'Dear passengers…'

There was a long period of silence.

Plov shifted in his seat and glanced out at the snowbound runway. A fleet of heavy Antonovs stood under heavy duvets of snow, standing like a pack of wolves at the ready. Plov adjusted his glasses as he scanned his eye down the fuselage of the plane. Two workmen, standing on top of a ladder, had taken away the outer casing of the starboard engine and were prodding at some wires inside.

Plov sighed.

He was unconcerned. The Tupolovs were manufactured in Uzbekistan and the engineers on the ground were some of the best in the world. Indeed, the Tupolov was the best in the world. It was only unfortunate that the planes were allowed to get so old. Things mechanical gave up in the end, however well built and well maintained they were. The heavy tail fin, with the three engines, attached right on the back, were bound to fall off when the plane decided it had just had enough. It was possible to see the remains of burnt out Tupolov tailplanes, the holy trinity of the three rear mounted engines staring up at you as you flew over them.

How has it all gone so wrong?

The best social system in the world, replaced… by what?

The men outside were poking about and discussing what to do. Then they replaced the casing, screwed on a couple of bolts and gave the thumbs up.

Chocks away! The tow truck started heaving the heavy plane away from its snow encrusted bay towards the runway.

Bumping over the uneven surface Plov dozed, scattered memories of his recent stay in the US came back to him.

He was at the airport being greeted – along with Mr Osman, the cousin of the President who was there to keep an eye on him. This same Mr Osman was now seated, legs akimbo spreading over seats 1A and 1B. He looked like a turnip sitting there, a big wide middle sloshing around with whisky, and the remains of hamburgers.

After a few minutes the engines started first time, and the plane began its lumbering approach to the runway.

'Dr Plov, your Excellency. Mr Osman, how good to see you again!'

Plov had bowed stiffly from the waist while Osman had gone in for an expansive bear hug. Well, he had polished off several miniatures of vodka from the stewardess' tray on the way over. They climbed into a limo with two of their US counterparts.

There was not one of the usual introductory pleasantries that Plov had come to expect, no asking after wives or girlfriends. One of them told him:

'Wife? Heck I don't even have time to date never mind marry!'

Once in the car, one of the Americans, a young man with a crew cut, sitting close to Plov, opened his laptop and, with his mobile interrupting the conversation, proceeded to have a meeting there and then in the back of the car.

The other guy, sitting with Osman, never stopped yapping away.

'Do you kind of mind if we go through a few points, Dr Plov, about the speech you are going to give at the World Bank tomorrow? It might be helpful...would you excuse me while I take that call?'

What a way to conduct a conversation – in snatches!

When the man got off the phone he had lost his train of thought

'The speech tomorrow...'

'Yes,' Plov acknowledged.

Bling bling!

'I'm sorry…'

Plov gestured politely for him to take the call, and the other American snapped his clam phone together and started to brief Plov. But, he talked so quickly that Plov could not understand a word he uttered.

They were taken downtown to New York. The hotel was good. Not that much better than the Dedeman Silk Road in Taskhent, but five times more expensive, at least. And everyone wanted a tip. There was even a performance at the airport when the taxi driver claimed there were too many suitcases for his vehicle. He demanded a second car be brought over. Then the drivers could not agree on the same price to the hotel. They wanted a tip just to heave the cases into the cars. It was outrageous and rude, Plov thought.

Still, as plenipotentiary and speaker at the Free Trade and Privatisation Convention, Plov didn't have to pay. His hosts pleaded with the taxi drivers like suppliants at the shrine of the vestal virgin, it was unbelievable. The sight of two men dressed in smart suits begging with what to Plov looked like criminals from Sing Sing wearing grubby tee shirts and oil-stained jeans. Refugees off a banana boat they were, black as the ace of spades with pineapple faces to boot.

The Americans dropped them at their hotel and promised to be back later. Plov got the very distinct impression that he was onerous to them, a lumbering technocrat from the soviet era that they were attempting to brainwash with the free-market doctrine. But Plov knew that he would never be convinced, not because he thought the free market was wrong, but because these Americans had no idea what it was like in his country. They had no clue at all as to what was going on.

Plov detested their easy superiority, and felt his patriotism surge in direct relation to the men's litany of praise about the American way of life. Their easy assumption that America was the best country in the world irked Plov. The good doctor smiled grimly to himself at the American's naivety in thinking their doctrine could be imported to Uzbekistan without a hitch. They had no idea what it was like at all; the daily struggles, the illegal use of force, the extortion, the daily grind of people's lives, and the exactions of the state; the casual drop-by visits by functionaries demanding bribes, or even taking over small businesses as soon as they were viable… no, these Americans thought everything was the way it was like in the US; supercharged speed, processed food, processed sex, without any human understanding at all.

Plov was not going to play along. When the porter left his luggage in his room he merely said thank you and goodnight.

That evening, the men had presented Plov and Osman with gold American Express Cards, with a $100,000 limit. Osman's face lit up and he thanked the Americans profusely bobbing his head again and again over his Martini cocktail. Plov still had his in his pocket; he would shred it when he got to Tashkent. Plov's soul was not for sale.

So, now they were on the runway and the plane was taxiing to the take off point. Ahead of them was a Boeing flown by US Airways. It looked gleaming compared to the smoke encrusted Tupolov. Their planes now were directed alongside each other to wait for a landing slot, and each passenger could view the other, each pilot his counterpart through the porthole windows.

Plov was sitting in business class. The captain came out to inspect the problematic engine through the window of seat number 45A. In so doing he left the door to the cockpit open.

Plov could see right through to the antediluvian flight deck. At once the radio crackled and an American voice could be heard.

'Say guys! How ya doing? Heard you had engine trouble back there. I don't want to alarm you, but did you know your starboard engine is leaking fluid? Over.'

There was a pause. The co-pilot sat limply in his seat and waited for the captain to double back. This he did, with a face like granite, holding on to the tops of the chairs as he came.

The American pilot carried on.

'I've made an official request to the control tower....'

The captain made it to the flight desk and closed the door.

A few minutes later, both planes were still on the runway, alongside each other, the Boeing and Tupolov 154M. Snow was falling.

The tannoy crackled.

'Dear Passengers. This is your Captain speaking. We are waiting for clearance to take off. There is a delay because the captain of the American Airline Boeing wishes to make a detour. He has offered to take you on the Boeing to Tashkent as mercy mission. I have told him we do not need such a gesture. It is provocative. I have told him that no passenger wishes to fly in his Boeing to Tashkent. We are Uzbek airline! We are ready to fly! If anyone does not agree, please make your name known to cabin staff. Thank you.'

The Russian words were translated into English and broadcast but most quickly understood what was going on.

The passengers rose up as one body and reached up for the hand luggage, putting on their overcoats, coughing, talking and rubbing their hands.

It looked as if the entire aircraft were ready to decamp. Not Plov. He remained seated.

Steps had been rushed to the plane, the doors opened and the passengers disembarked. No one noticed that Plov had not left.

The captain opened the flight deck door and jerked back on the soles of his feet when he saw Plov planted in his seat.

'Time to disembark,' he said.

'Fly me to Tashkent!' Plov said.

'How can I do that? You are the only passenger!'

'Fly me to Tashkent!' he ordered.

The captain and his co-pilot sat down with Plov and opened up some of Plov's duty free that he brought down from the overhead lockers.

Together they spoke of many things. Plov related his entire American experience and how, when he got to Tashkent he was going to introduce privatisation. Next to them the Boeing's engines started up and the plane moved on the runway. Then, with a roar, it took off.

'Not bad,' said the captain.

'You fly better,' said Plov.

After they finished the brandy, the captain received clearance for take-off.

The flight was faultless. On arrival, they learnt that the Boeing had, in contrast, overshot the runway by some margin. The American pilots, unused to the icy conditions, had made a mess of it. All passengers were unhurt, however. They were all clustered in the arrivals hall and watched the Tupolov come down perfectly, without even a bump.

Now that was flying!

When Plov appeared at the door, he found the entire airport staff lined up, their hands coming together in applause.

It was a heady moment, and the colour rushed to his cheeks. He savoured the moment. After all, he knew that his next words would be received in disdainful silence.

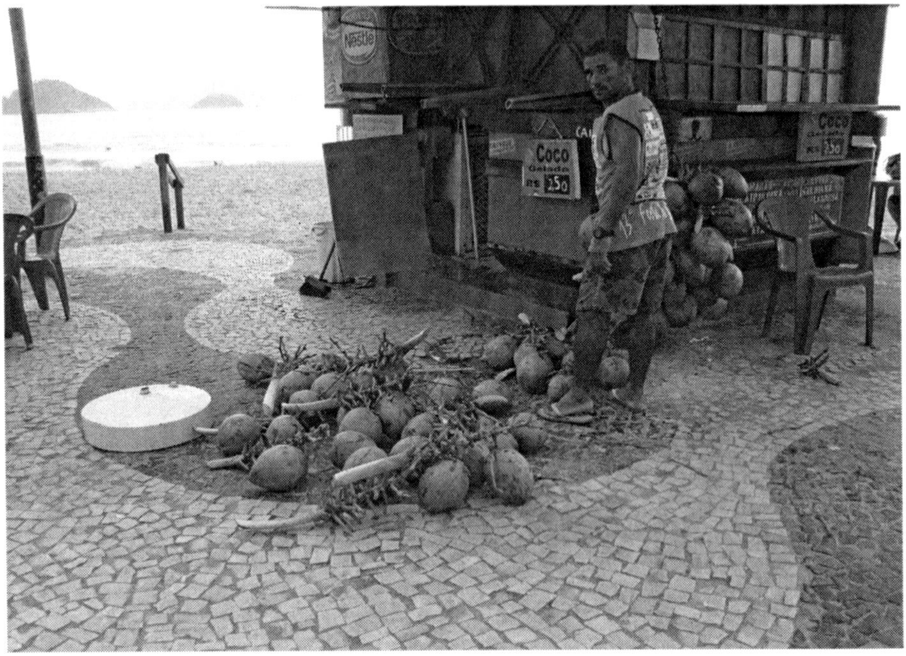
Nestlé
Coco
Gelado
R$ 2.50
Coco

Printed in the United Kingdom by
Lightning Source UK Ltd., Milton Keynes
140581UK00001B/44/P